JAMAICAN Witchcraft

The Reluctant Obeah Man and Other Stories

DAVID BRAILSFORD

Illustrated by John Stilgoe

All LMH titles, imprints and distributed lines are available at special quantity discounts for bulk purchases for sales promotion, premiums, fund-raising, educational or institutional use.

Cover Design: Sanya Dockery
Edited by: Nicola Brown
Book Design, Layout &Typset: Sanya Dockery

Published by: LMH Publishing Limited
7 Norman Road,
LOJ Industrial Complex
Suite 10-11
Kingston C.S.O., Jamaica
Tel: 876-938-0005; 938-0712
Fax: 876-759-8752
Email: lmhbookpublishing@cwjamaica.com
Website: www.lmhpublishing.com

Printed in the U.S.A.   ISBN: 978-976-8202-61-1

DEDICATED TO MY DEAR WIFE LEONIE

Contents

Acknowledgements

Introduction

The Medallion   1

Rattle, Rattle   11

De Lawrence Fire   19

Did you know? (1)   27

Power over the Mind   31

Get to the Heart of the Matter   35

Doubting Thomas   45

Bell, Book and Candle   53

Did you know? (2)   65

The Reluctant Obeah man   69

The Stubborn Duppies   77

Maggoty, Maggoty   87

Never look back   93

Did you know? (3)   101

Come-Uppance   105

Tricks of the Trade   111

The Rivals   113

To divert the course of Justice   117

An English Obeah Story   127

Did you know? (4)   133

Cock on a Stick   137

The Will   143

Conclusion   153

Notes   155

About the Author/Illustrator   163

Acknowledgements

To those who have sown a seed for a good tale.

To the National Library of Jamaica for their wonderful resources.

To my daughter, Marie, for her help with word processing.

To my dear wife, Leonie, for her advice with the Jamaican patois.

To my friend at the Jamaican Women's Dinner Club, for Doubting Thomas and The Stubborn Duppies.

To Evelyn for The Rivals.

To my good friends at the Nottingham Storytellers Club who have encouraged me so much.

To the members of the Eastwood Writers Club who have taught me so much.

Another special thanks to John Stilgoe for his wonderful illustrations.

To my publisher, Mike Henry, and his team who have brought my book to life.

Introduction

What is this witchcraft in Jamaica that they call Obeah? We know that it has its roots deep in folk religion from Africa and in spite of being an illegal practice, it still prospers and the people visit Obeah men and women when they require advice regarding health problems, both physical and psychological.

Like other such religions that recommend being 'in balance' with nature and the environment, Obeah offers the holistic approach to personal well being, utilising traditional herbal medicine and common sense counselling.

But added to this is a magical element.

The word is associated with occult powers, wizardry and sorcery, so although one aspect of the practice is herbalistic, the lotions and potions are supposedly given additional potency by the use of rituals, spells and amulets.

This knowledge was carried to the lush islands of Jamaica and Trinidad and Tobago over 200 years ago, during the dreadful years of slavery, but still has around it a cloak of secrecy and fear.

Unlike my book about ghosts, entitled **Duppy Stories**, the sorting of fact from fiction has been difficult. I found, in the first instance, that the populace revelled in telling traditional tales about ghosts and enjoyed recounting their own meetings with mischievous duppies. This folklore is still expressed by exchanging stories about 'things that go bump in the night,' when folks gather at 'nine-nights' to pay respect and say 'goodbye' to their beloved family member or friend who has passed over to Jesus.

Mention of Obeah, however, tends to cause an immediate cessation of conversation and when pressed, produces remarks like:

"We don't talk about such things!" or "I'm a Christian!"

This response caused me some confusion, for I found on occasions, that some of those who reacted in this way, claiming that their Pastor would not approve, sometimes turn to Obeah practitioners for advice. This ability to merge apparently opposing forces of belief is not uncommon, as can be seen by the fusion of African belief in magic with Catholicism to produce Voodoo; and in some parts of the West Indies, Obeah has intermingled with the Muslim faith.

Recently, back home in England, I found a leaflet at my front door from a certain Madam, who was advertising her services as a healer, claiming to be a practitioner of root and herb medicine, offering spiritual baths and being able to remove the evil influences of black magic, Obeah, Jadoo and Unganga.

An Obeah woman to be sure, so I rang her hoping for an interview so that she could give me some insight into this art of witchcraft. She cut me dead with, "My religion will not permit my activities to be written down for publication!"

I bet it won't!

Similarities in practice can be seen with the Marabout, who advertise regularly in the Jamaican press in England, claiming to be able to solve all of your problems surrounding love, work, bad luck, impotence, success, domestic and marital disputes, ridding victims of evil forces and repelling witchcraft by using powerful spells.

They were originally Muslim holy people, who wandered about the country-side in Africa, offering spiritual guidance, arbitrating in disputes, working miracles and dispensing magical amulets.

Obeah may have links with Shamanism and other forms of witchcraft and certainly claims to have influence over the spirits of the dead; however the path of the Obeah is difficult to trace.

Running parallel with Obeah practice is Myalism or Mialism and Pocomanism, which are purported to be the 'white' aspect of the craft. These people work to cast out the evil workings of the Obeah and are recognised by their Myal dancing. Much could be said about the Myal, or 'four eyes', but to simplify the contents of this book, we will consider that in practical terms the activities merge. Moreover, the term is less common than Obeah.

It is said that Obeah men and women are skilled in the use of poisons, not being averse to accepting contracts to eliminate a rival when their client is in conflict with neighbours. Many cases of Obeah poisoning can be found in the annals of Jamaican history.

One belief that is firm in Jamaica is that Obeah has power over the ghosts of dead people. It has the ability to change them into all manner of creatures such as snakes, alligators, crocodiles, frogs and lizards, which may then be sent to torment and harm the living. When under such threat, you will need to wear amulets or invoke spells to drive away these mischievous duppies. Counter magic will be obtained from another Obeah man or woman, making the whole thing a lucrative business.

Not surprisingly, authentic handbooks about the actual practice of Obeah magic are unavailable on the shelves of reputable high street book shops, so it is difficult to ascertain how much of Voodoo, Shamanism and other Afro-Witchcraft are part of the Jamaican scene.

Do Obeah practitioners stick pins into hexing dolls to inflict pain on their chosen victims? Do they burn black candles? Do they make blood offerings? Do they chant or recite secret incantations to make their charms? Do they make amulets of folded paper, on which are written magical words that are to be worn around the neck for a specified time and then thrown backwards into a stream at night, carrying with them unwanted ailments? Do they obtain pieces of hair, nail clippings or articles of clothing and perform Relantum rituals over them to facilitate an attack, causing injury to the owner at a distance? As sooth-sayers, do they interpret dreams, signs and omens? What power do they actually hold over the spirits of the dead?

Once again, this white man, born and bred in Nottingham, England has decided to venture into the dark bush of Jamaica, to capture stories – authentic and imaginary – about this secretive practice of Obeah, to find out why it is both feared and sought after by elements of the population. As with the stories of duppies, I find that some experiences are close to the family of my Jamaican born wife, Leonie, but she is of the opinion that much of the practice is just trickery, used to control and make a questionable living out of gullible and superstitious residents.

Have you the courage to accompany me on a safari to find and investigate this hidden, secret world of witchcraft?

The Medallion

Two brothers lived with their ailing father on a small holding of land close by Mitchell Town in Vere, Clarendon. Nathaniel, the elder brother, was well liked by the neighbours. He was a gentle God-fearing boy who loved his invalid father and had been the corner stone of the family since his mother died.

Six years earlier papa had been smitten by a stroke, so Nathaniel found himself nursing his father and maintaining the house, as well as working the land to provide a livelihood. Times were hard but he never complained, even though his younger brother, Logan, never lifted a finger to help. Nathaniel was indeed such an upstanding boy that he became the regular target of young women who saw in him the makings of an ideal husband.

Logan, however, was not impressed. He had always been jealous of Nathaniel, and had resented him since childhood because Nathaniel had been more successful at school. According to the teachers, Logan was a lazy good-for-nothing truant who would never become anything good.

They were right. He would never be a match for his industrious brother. He was just a parasite, begging from the long-suffering Nathaniel, from strangers and from friends. From time to time he would join in some nefarious scheme being cooked up by his criminal associates, but not a dollar of his ill-gotten gains ever found its way back to support his father. Whenever he did have a wad of money, it was invariably spent on loose women, rum, and gold jewellery, the latter obsession giving him the nickname 'Goldie' amongst his drinking pals.

On every finger and each thumb Logan sported a flashy gold ring and he wore numerous gold chains around his neck; a gaudy crucifix, a garish St. Christopher and a large medallion engraved with the Jamaican Coat of Arms.

As he tried to live the high life, his out-goings constantly exceeded his income, so he began to brood on the possibility of profiting from the sale of his father's estate, saying to himself, [1] "Mi waan di two a dem fi ded!"

This wishful thinking soon became an obsession and he started to plan ways of disposing of his father and Nathaniel, so that he could inherit the house and land.

How about taking a cutlass to them one night and blaming a burglar? But how would he provide a solid alibi? Maybe he could pay a friend to carry out the heinous deed, but who could he trust?

Many an evening he would sit alone in the local bar, rehearsing in his mind's eye the new lifestyle that he could enjoy once he had the money for his carousing, but on one particular occasion, his attention was drawn to two of his cronies who were propping up the bar and swapping jokes and stories about the local Obeah man.

[2] "Ah, di Obeah man!" Logan reasoned, [3] "Mi a go si di Obeah man an' si if 'im wi 'elp mi!"

Fortified by a couple of glasses of rum, he ventured out into the darkness and set off for the Obeah man's house, leaving the comforting bar lights and heading up the lane, until his mind was immediately swamped with frightening images of duppies, demons and night monsters. The very trees seemed to be alive, stretching out their branches like grasping arms, snaring his progress.

He was sure he could hear night creatures call his name, but spurred on by the thought of future prosperity, he persevered.

A difficult moment came as he approached the thick bush that surrounded the Obeah man's hut but, turning off the familiar lane, he forced himself to plunge into the undergrowth.

A glimmer of light drew him on and finally he reached the rickety gate that led into the yard of an old colonial style house.

The gate protested with a groan as Logan entered and then it slammed shut behind him with startling force. As he stood composing himself, a voice rang out from inside the old house, [4]"A who dat?"

Logan froze.

He was frightened. No doubt about it, he was frightened!

The front door swung open and a shaft of light flooded the yard, illuminating the spot where he stood shaking, his eyes rolling white at the sight of the man who advanced onto the veranda.

[5]"Wha yu waant! Wha yu cum fa?"

The Obeah man was tall, very black and peered down at Logan with dark searching eyes.

Logan stuttered his name, then raised enough courage to blurt out his business.

[6]"Yu know wha yu ask fa? Yu know wha yu ask mi fi do?" queried the magic man as the two of them settled on the rocking chair on the veranda. [7] "It serious, yu know!"

[8] "Yes, mi noa!" Logan replied, "But yu wi get moni wen mi 'ouse sell!"

An hour passed, during which time the Obeah man and Logan discussed the best way to dispose of the father and brother. Logan eventually left with a phial of liquid poison. Just a few drops would be more than enough to send his family to eternal rest.

With a handshake to seal the agreement, Logan headed for home.

It took him many days to rouse himself enough to set about his cowardly deed but one overcast Monday evening, just before supper time, he stealthily made his way to his father's yard.

All was quiet and deserted. Father would be dozing in his bedroom and Nathaniel was nowhere to be seen.

From where he hid behind the perimeter wall, he could see into the outside kitchen where, on a wood fire, a Dutch pot full of simmering soup was ready for the evening meal.

Logan crept from behind the wall and made *for* the kitchen.

Without warning, he was berated by loud barking. He had forgotten the dogs, especially the pack leader, Ben.

Ben snapped at Logan's feet until a well placed kick sent the dog flying into the air. The rest of the dogs withdrew, tails between their legs.

With a furtive look around, in case the rumpus had attracted attention, Logan pressed on into the kitchen, took out the phial and released its deadly contents into the soup. He hurried back to wait in the bush.

It wasn't long before Nathaniel arrived, carrying a large juicy looking melon that would round off supper. Logan watched him ladle out two bowls of soup and then vanish into the house, calling out to father that supper was ready.

It was another two hours before Logan dared to come out of hiding and make his way across the yard, waving a switch to silence the dogs, up the veranda steps and into the silent house.

[9] "Papa! Nathaniel! Whe uno de?"

No answer. He advanced towards the only light, a faint glow in the back bedroom. All was ominously still. The sound of his heart beating was so loud it seemed to resonate through the rafters. Sidling into the bedroom he saw the dreadful result of what he had done. His father lay on the bed. His brother Nathaniel was slumped in the rocking chair with one arm hanging down to the floor. An empty soup bowl stood in a pool of vomit on the wooden boards. Clearly, both had come to a ghastly end, their faces contorted by the effect of the Obeah man's virulent poison. For a moment, Logan froze, then fled to empty the contents of his stomach onto the yard.

He leant against the porch railing, retched again and again at the thought of his vile deed, and it was some time before he was able to pull himself together enough to set about the grizzly task of disposing of the evidence.

Grunting, he dragged the grimacing corpses from the house, loaded them onto a cart and covered them with a tarpaulin. Satisfied that the bodies were completely covered, he went back into the house to wash the bowls, Dutch pot and utensils and scrub away at them to remove every vestige of the poison. When that was done, he mopped the floor to remove any excretions that might betray him. Working harder than he had ever done before in his life, he dragged the cart through the yard and onto a remote part of the district, deep in the bush, where he dug a shallow grave. It was a struggle to move the stiffening corpses, who seemed to be resisting his efforts to hide them. Even in death, his father's bony fingers clutched at the gold chains around Logan's throat.

The bodies were roughly dumped head to feet into the trench, covered over with bauxite red earth, and all signs of the cart's track marks brushed away.

An hour later he was drinking at the bar with his pals and the following day he calmly swaggered into the local Police Station to make a missing person's report.

[10] "Mi go 'ome dis marnin', an' mi noa si mi bredda nar mi papa. Mi luk ebery weh, but mi caant fine dem. Papa cyaan walk, so w'appen? Dis a baffle mi!"

This set the law in motion, but enquiries at the hospital and around the district produced nothing. The investigation seemed to be never ending; numerous neighbours being cross examined in an effort to shed light on this mysterious disappearance but to no avail. Logan was subjected to interview after interview by the constabulary, but he remained cool and let nothing slip.

Some five months passed, then the missing persons file was put to one side. Logan moved into the family house, gloating to himself that he had gotten away with it. He would let the gossip die down for a few more months, then sell the house and land and live things up with his mates as planned.

CRBOEOQR

Constable Henry Robertson pressed down hard onto the pedals of his trusty bicycle. His day at work had been uneventful and he would soon be devouring some curried goat that his wife, Muriel, had promised him as he left home that morning. As he approached a steep gradient, his bike became more resistant to his touch, until he was compelled to dismount, standing for a moment to catch his breath and wipe sweat from his brow.

Suddenly from somewhere deep in the bush, his ears were beset by a most mournful howling. He was accustomed to the barking of yard dogs as he passed by his neighbours' yards, but this was something else. The plaintive cry rose high into the air and night creatures ceased their chatter. Henry stood for a moment to identify the sound, then shook his head and stepped onto the pedal to remount.

"AaaaooooOOOOHHH!"

There it was again! The sound of an animal in great distress.

"AAaaaaoooooOOOOOHHH!"

What on earth could it be? What in Jehovah's creation could make such a din?

Henry knew that he could not go home without finding the source of this, so leaning the bike against a tree, he entered the bush.

It was creepy in there! An owl had regained its voice and was joined by a chorus of crickets. Trees stirred in a rising breeze, moaning and creaking, their moving shadows giving a fleeting impression of figures creeping through the undergrowth.

Constable Henry was none too keen to be wandering about in the habitat of duppies but he was determined to find the source of the unholy sounds.

It was close by now and, as Henry broke out into a small clearing, he saw a large dog sitting on its haunches, baying at the moon. The paws and jowls of the creature were covered in red soil, as though it had been digging.

There, in front of it, in the recently disturbed soil, a putrefying human hand raised two fingers to the heavens.

ᄋᔜᄋᔔᄋᔕ

Protecting their noses with handkerchiefs, the local constabulary dug up the gruesome rotting remains of Nathaniel and his father. Spade by spade full of soil was carefully removed from the stinking corpses, until Logan's family was in full view.

As they peered down into the shallow grave, an object glimmered in the light of the full moon. Sergeant Henry bent over and carefully released it from the bony fingers of one of the dead men. It was covered in soil, but a quick shake revealed a thick gold chain and a large medallion...

...a medallion displaying the Jamaican Coat of Arms.

"...a putrefying human hand raised two fingers to the heavens."

Rattle, Rattle

It is widely believed in Jamaica that if you wish to hurt your enemies, then go to see an Obeah man. Using magic, he will send a duppy or ghost who will haunt them by throwing stones onto their roof at night and the only way that they can deal with this jinx, is to obtain a counter spell from another 'science man'.

⋇⋇⋇⋇⋇

Rattle, rattle... there it goes again.

Somebody throwing stones onto the roof.

Bertha tossed back the sheet, swung her weary legs out of bed and, muttering to herself, tiptoed to the window. Once again some-one, or something, had come to her old house in the early hours of the morning bent on mischief, but she could see no-one outside.

Born in 1930, Bertha had spent all her life in this family house in Cuffie Head, Portland. Never before had she been subjected to such duppy nonsense, to such a terrible din which had tormented her every night for a week. Each time she heard the clatter of hard objects raining down on her corrugated zinc roof, she dragged herself into the lane, crying, [1] "A who a trow sinting pan mi roof?"

She would walk up and down the lane and scout around the house but no-one was to be seen. Again she would call out, [2]"If mi eber ketch uno, uno a go si wha mi a go do uno!" No-one replied.

[3]"Smadi a try fi Obeah mi, but mi no ca 'ow im try, im cyaan get tru!"

Grumbling to herself, Bertha would return to her bed and suffer a restless night. The moment dawn broke, she would be back in the yard, checking out the roof. Nothing. Not a single object or stone.

So this was what Bertha decided to do. After a quick breakfast of fried plantain, she set out to visit her local sorcerer and was soon taking her place in his waiting room. When her turn came, she was ushered into the consulting room, where she was greeted by an elderly, fat bellied man, who peered at her over the flat topped rims of old fashioned spectacles.

Bertha felt uneasy.

Between Bertha and the Obeah man there was a low table covered with a pristine white lace tablecloth. In the centre of the table there was an ancient well thumbed copy of the Bible, and at one end an arrangement of fruits. A selection of amulets, some crucifix pendants and a collection of finger rings were at the other end.

"Tek a seat mi dear. Wha yu cum fa?"

[4]"Ebery nite stones rackle pan mi roof an mi no like it."

A sly smile crept over his pock-marked features.

[5]"Duppy know who fi frighten, but mi ab di cure fi dat."

He walked across the bare wooden floor to an old cupboard, half opened the door and rummaged around. He returned to

Bertha holding a small piece of parchment paper and sat down on the other side of the table. For some time they discussed her problem, making the occasional reference to the Scriptures, and Bertha watched as he wrote some seemingly foreign words on the parchment, folded it and handed it over.

[6] "Put dis inna yu wallet. Mine now, no laas it, an eberyting wi arite. Five hundred dollar is mi fee."

Without comment, Bertha paid her dues, nodded her farewell and made her way home. She had no doubt that her torment would soon be over.

After supper she retired early to catch up on some sleep and having placed the parchment as directed, she was soon fast off.

All went well until an hour or two after midnight.

Rattle, rattle, rattle.

[7] "Wha! Nat agen?"

With a groan of despair, she leapt out of bed, grabbed a broom and rushed out into the yard. Once again there was no back to beat with her heavy broom, and other than the hoot of a distant owl, there wasn't a sound, not even the slightest rustling that might betray a prowler.

Enough was enough.

With no thought for her appearance, she ran all the way to the Obeah man's house and banged loudly on his door. It took some time to arouse him, but eventually she heard the shuffling and grunting of someone coming down the passage. The door bolt grated, the door creaked open and the Obeah man's sleepy voice said, [8] "Who a lik dung mi doar an a mek s'much nize?"

"...she sprinkled a large circle of powder around her yard."

[9] "Its me! Berta Johnson! Mi hav a writ 'gainst yuh man. Mi paye 'yu mi heapa moni fi wuk fi mi an nuttin no appen."

The door opened a fraction more.

[10] "Nuh badda mi, woman. Yu noa wha time dis?"

[11] "Mi beg yuh fi gimme a 'han wid mi problem."

[12] "Oh! A yu miss. Mi get upset when smaddy mek nize a mi doar, an mi no noa a who. Cum in Miss Berta."

"Tank yuh sah."

With much gesticulating, Bertha declared that the outrage was continuing.

[13] "Dat magic mussy too trang. Yuh need special magic fram mi."

From his cupboard, he took an old black box which he laid with due reverence on the offerings table. The lid was raised to reveal a moist, musty-smelling black powder, which he scooped out until he had filled a small canvas pouch. Drawing the string to seal the neck, he placed the pouch in Bertha's hand.

[14] "Sprinkle dis roun yuh 'ouse an nutten wi come close. Five hundred dollar is mi fee."

With noticeable reluctance, she paid up and shuffled her way home, complaining bitterly to herself but still clutching the purse of black powder. Surely this would drive away those malevolent spirits.

Back at the house, putting all her faith in the magic, she sprinkled a large circle of powder around her yard.

"Dat wi do it!"

With a long sigh, she slid into bed, pulled up the sheet and after prayers, fell asleep.

Rattle, Rattle, Rattle.

Bertha screamed, leapt up, and stormed around the house calling down a curse from heaven to inflict the prankster with boils, lice and some latter day ailments that would have horrified even Pharaoh.

As dawn broke, she was still locked into the furious back and forth, back and forth rhythm of her trusty rocking chair, angrily cussing and grumbling about the unknown enemy who was tormenting her.

[15] "Di Obeah man cyaan 'elp mi. Mi haffi ketch di wickid spirit."

No sooner had she thought it than she was up and dressed and went down the lane to recruit her two sons.

Big boys they were.

When she had told them the story of her persecution she said, [16] "Mi waan yuh fi 'ide inna di bush near di yard an ketch anybady wi mek mischif an beat im."

The next midnight found her two sons well concealed in the undergrowth and on the lookout for the trouble maker.

For two hours they crouched, watching in the moonlight and listening to the night breezes whispering amongst the trees, until their imaginations began to conjure up lurking figures everywhere they looked. Twice they rushed out into the lane, convinced that someone was pussyfooting in Bertha's yard, only to find that it was shadows cast by the old Cottonwood tree.

They were close to abandoning their vigil and heading for home when a sound caught their attention. Someone was approaching from down the lane. Backing into a thick growth of shrubs, they stood motionless, eyes fixed on the brow of the hill, where a shadowy figure was coming into view. Head and shoulders bent forward, he carried a large and obviously heavy bucket which was placed quietly down just outside Bertha's gate. Peering from side to side, the man dipped into the bucket and hurled something that glinted in the faint light of the moon as it landed - *rattle, rattle* - and rolled -*rattle, rattle* - down the zinc roof.

It was ice. Cubes of ice that were thrown handful after handful to create the terrible racket that had been waking poor Bertha.

No wonder that nothing was ever found the following morning.

As Bertha began to rant and rave in her bedroom, the intruder ran to shelter in the bush, but they were faster and pounced with shrieks of triumph.

The man let out a wail, writhed and squirmed and struggled to evade capture, but the boys held on tight and started beating him, again and again. Like a punch bag, he was knocked backwards and forwards from one to the other. They had no mercy.

"Mama, Mama! Cum! Wi ketch im!"

Bertha ran out onto the porch while the boys dragged her tormentor to meet her.

"Mek mi si yuh, yuh bitch yuh," she screeched and screamed and grabbing his hair, forced him to face the light.

It was as if she had been stung by a wasp and she jumped back in shock. Bertha stepped back with a puzzled expression on her face and cried out, [17] "Obeah man! Obeah man! A weh yuh a do yah?"

De Lawrence Fire

Power is often wielded over the superstitious minded by occult societies using clandestine knowledge.

Such a society is the De Lawrence or De Laurance, an organisation so covert that one cannot find its name written down in order to ascertain the spelling.

The advertising of their wares has been banned in many parts of the world but, if you require charms, rings or amulets to bring prosperity or ward off evil, then there are those who know the way to this secret world of magic.

Research into this Obeah-like activity is difficult, because initiates, fearing recrimination, tend to keep their mouths sealed.

The following story is based on a series of events that were reported to have happened in Manchester, England, some time in the early seventies.

ॐ৪০৪০৪

Esmie was doing very well for herself, but earlier days had been hard before she met De Lawrence.

She had come to England with her husband in 1958, leaving her poor life in Trenchtown, Jamaica, to search for better things in the British Isles.

Relatives who were already settled in Manchester had made them welcome, and had given them support, as they struggled to get a toe-hold in the local economy.

Before things began to look up, however, Esmie's husband had taken sick and died. Her grief was soon followed by homesickness and she found it difficult to throw off self pity. Still wrapped in a cloak of mourning, Esmie went back to her work as a domestic at a local hospital. She was a proud woman and the need to be independent of her kind relatives soon led her to a ground-floor, one-room flat in a large four-storey urban house in a cosmopolitan area of town. Things were primitive. No carpet and just one tattered chair and a second-hand single bed on which to rest her weary legs after work. Her cooker and sink were also in the one room while a shared bathroom was on the landing above. Her Aunt Angela popped in from time to time to offer encouragement and gossip.

[1] "How yuh do Esmie? Yuh mus be lonely!"

[2] "Mi ante, mi a manage, but mi miss Lester!"

[3] "Mi si! Yuh know dat yuh can cum to si mi any time yuh waan!"
Esmie smiled a wry smile.

[4] "Mi a get use to mi lickle flat, an mi a manage, tank yuh!"

[5] "Arite! But yuh no figet whe mi sey now!"

There was a pause, then Esmie said quietly, [6] "Eben doah tings bad bak a Jamaica, mi ome sick, yuh si. If mi could only afford di flight!"

[7] "We woulda like fi elp, Esmie. Yu waan go a De Lawrence. It wi elp yuh, yuh know".

[8] "Oh! Obeah yuh mean! Why mi neva tink a dat?"

[9] "Mi wi contak dem if yuh waan!"

"Arite den!"

So, with her aunt's help, Esmie made contact with the De Lawrence and committed herself to paying a monthly amount in exchange for a prosperity amulet.

Almost immediately things improved.

She was offered a supervisor's post at work and, every Thursday night, without fail, she had a big win at the local Bingo Palace. Then a friend of a friend offered her part time work which further improved her new found prosperity.

So, for many months to come, she was able to put money aside for the day that she would fly home. She made some improvements to her living environment, but she also bought many personal items to carry back to Jamaica.

She kept them all in a large trunk which stood at the foot of her bed, the kind of trunk that Jamaicans were prone to keep at that time, and every night everything was unpacked, checked, refolded and re-packed with loving care.

For three whole years Esmie performed this ritual, her savings mounted and she saw herself, in her imagination, flying over the Atlantic Ocean. Six more months should do it but, the closer she came to her ambition, the more remiss Esmie became in keeping her promise to pay the De Lawrence each month.

She received warnings of dire consequence, but she took no heed.

One cold, wet evening in November, Esmie was at the trunk, checking her prized possessions. Many of her fellow tenants were cloistered in their rooms, huddled in front of their small gas fires, gratefully warming their toes as they listened to the rain spattering against the single-glazed windows.

Louis Brown, who lived on the top floor, reluctantly prepared to go to start his shift as night watchman at the Council's Work Yard. Donning a warm high-necked pullover and collecting his industrial raincoat and torch, he left his room, pausing only to secure his door, then slowly descended the stairs, landing by landing. With a final adjustment to his coat, he opened the front door and prepared to step out into the street but, there before him, hovering head-high, was a ball of fire. Small, only as big as his fist, but it was there alright, causing Louis to step back in alarm.

It looked for all the world like a miniature sun. A small red sun with swirling red flames flickering from its surface. But Louis could feel no heat so, with palm forwards, he slowly raised his hand and cautiously moved it closer, until it nearly touched the flames. He let his hand pass right through and felt nothing. No heat, no pain, nothing.

[10] "Lawd mi Gad! A wha dis!"

Louis quickly stepped aside as the ball floated pass his head and entered the lobby. Whirling around, he was just in time to see it gliding back and forth before it ascended the staircase.

"Wha yuh afta!" he whispered as though he expected the thing to reply.

One flight, two flights, three flights it went, right up to the top landing where it passed through the door of flat number seven.

Louis waited for an ensuing commotion but his neighbour must have been out for all remained quiet. His ears strained to

"...he slowly raised his hand...until it nearly touched the flames"

pick up any tell-tale sound and a few tense minutes passed by before the glowing ball emerged, with no apparent harm to the solid timber door. Gliding silently on, it crossed the landing and disappeared through Louis' own door.

Louis shouted, "Wha yuh afta, man?" and taking out his key as he ran, he raced up the stairs, unlocked his door and, panting heavily, he was inside his flat in seconds.

There it was, seemingly prying into every nook and cranny looking for the Lord knows what, then it went pass Louis, down the stairs to the third landing and into the next flat. The quiet was instantly shattered by a scream and the noise falling furniture. Louis flew down the stairs arriving just as the door burst open and a partly-dressed Sheila Jenkinson rushed out directly into his arms.

"Louis! There's something in my room!" she wailed.

The commotion brought an agitated response as more doors opened on the floor below and anxious faces peered curiously upwards towards the rumpus.

"Stay quiet!" Louis called down to his neighbours. "Someting funny going on up yah, but it naah cause trouble. Uno stay quiet!"

As he spoke the cold fire ball swept out from flat six and moved on to explore rooms five, four and so on down the stairs causing panic. Room after room were systematically searched as wide-eyed residents stepped aside, so as not to impede the passage of this strange intruder.

It reached the ground floor and approached the last room to be checked; a room that had originally been a dining or sitting room and was now the home of Esmie Robertson.

Esmie was, at that moment, kneeling by her bed, checking the contents of her trunk. The possessions she had obtained, thanks to the magic of De Lawrence. The De Lawrence with whom she had an agreement to pay for services rendered. An agreement that she had reneged upon and you don't go back on a promise to De Lawrence.

The fire-ball hovered outside her door.

The tenants had followed it down the stairway and were huddled and whispering together waiting for its next move. Louis called out, "Esmie! Open yuh door! We hav a visitor!"

The slow shuffling of slippered feet could be heard, then the door opened and dark eyes peeped out.

"Who dat?"

The fire suddenly became agitated, quivering excitedly and becoming brighter and, for the first time, incandescent. So hot, in fact, that all the neighbours backed away from its burning white heat.

"Lawd a merci!" Esmie threw open the door and retreated in terror.

With a fiery roar the ball of hot gas leapt forwards, made straight for the trunk and plunged in. The contents ignited immediately. Strangely, however, the wooden trunk itself didn't catch fire. It would seem that De Lawrence fire is single-minded in its mission to punish bad debtors and only items blessed by the amulet were to burn.

Esmie screamed and rushed forward to save what she could. It was not the intention of the messenger to harm Esmie, as it was only sent to avenge the bad debt by destroying her possessions, but, as she recklessly tried to beat out the flames, the fire leapt onto her night dress and she, too, was engulfed.

Louis rushed over, threw her to the ground and pulled the eiderdown from her bed to cover her and extinguish the blaze. He dragged her away from the trunk, but she was already critically injured and all that remained of her possessions was a wisp of smoke. Though Esmie was rushed to the hospital, all efforts to save her failed and she died a victim of De Lawrence ... or herself?

Perhaps after reading this account of events you will have learned an important lesson from Esmie's mistake...

... don't mess around with De Lawrence!

Obeah

That an Obeah practitioner can, with a simple movement of hand, silence the croaking frogs and command them to sing again with a whistle?

CRBOMOR

That they will cause death, by adding chopped up horse hair to dirt from a cemetery? This is then put into the food that a victim will eat, causing horrendous sores in the belly that will burst the bowels.

CRBOMOR

That Obeah is derived from an Ashanti word Obayifo? It also has origins in a Hebrew word meaning idol?

CRBOMOR

That if you hang up a bundle of sticks over your porch door it will ward off thieves?

CRBOMOR

That if some girls have an 'accident' and become pregnant, instead of acknowledging that a man is responsible, they will claim to have been obeah-ed?

႙ၹၦ႘ႃ

That higglers (market fruit sellers) engage Obeah men or women to guarantee that they will prosper?

႙ၹၦ႘ႃ

That Obeah men and women catch the shadows of living people and nail them to cotton wood trees?

႙ၹၦ႘ႃ

That if an Obeah 'doctor' throws graveyard dirt onto your roof, it will encourage duppies to 'rattle' around your yard? Only by taking the soil back will the mischief cease.

႙ၹၦ႘ႃ

That you can be poisoned via the skin as well as by the mouth? An Obeah man will soak the undergarments of an intended victim in a poisonous concoction that will then be absorbed through the skin to terminate life.

႙ၹၦ႘ႃ

That if you find a rusty nail hanging over your door, you will know that you have been obeah-ed? If you pass under it you will be afflicted or die.

ೞೞೞೞೞ

That if you find grave dirt in your bed, a feather in your pocket, or a dried lizard on your dinner plate, beware, it is likely you are being obeah-ed?

Power Over The Mind

Shirley is a strong character who would think nothing of jumping on the back of a motorbike taxi to take her down the Redberry Road into Porus, or to join in a game of dominoes with the men in their local bar.

She is in her seventies but takes no nonsense from any man, enjoys her life and is always forthright with her opinions.

Although a friend for many years, our paths do not often cross these days, for she spends her time travelling backwards and forwards between her house in Manchester, Jamaica and her other home in Florida, USA.

This short tale revolves around the shock that she received in coming home to find that her Jamaican house had been burgled. Someone had made a good job of it, for she no longer owned a refrigerator, deep-freezer, microwave, television, video and many other choice domestic items. Her response, though, was surprisingly calm, for she immediately knew how to recover her property and the following day, after breakfast, she made her way to Porus to spend the day gossiping with friends. Her first encounter was with Nancy.

"W'appen Shirley? Yuh back 'ome? 'Ow yuh du?"

[1] "Nat bad tanks, but mi na like 'ow smady rip mi aaf."

"... she made her way to Porus to spend the day gossiping..."

Nancy looked shocked.

[2] "Smady bruk yuh house? A wanda a who?"

[3] "Mi suspect smady, but if dem tink dem a get weh wid it dem mek a sad mistake."

"Wah di police seh?"

[4] "Police! Wah mi a tell police fa? A di Obeah man mi a go.'

Nancy looked down at the floor and went very quiet.

"Mi a go si Mister Brown an im wi fix dem."

Nancy made an excuse and left in a hurry.

Shirley smiled, for she knew that she had just tapped into the 'jungle telegraph,' it being well known in the district that Nancy could not hold on to juicy gossip. The news that Shirley was to visit the local Obeah man spread throughout the district like a forest fire.

She never did, of course, the 'word' was enough.

'Mind' magic had been invoked.

A week passed by whilst this threat of a curse festered amongst the criminal community.

Eight days after her meeting with Nancy, Shirley got out of bed, washed, dressed, had breakfast then went into the yard to feed the dogs. As she passed onto the veranda, a pleasant sight met her eyes, for there, all in a row, were her refrigerator, deep-freeze, microwave, television and video and her other choice domestic items.

Get To The Heart Of The Matter

Those of a delicate disposition should, perhaps, move on, for the following gruesome events, which took place somewhere in the parish of Manchester some time in the late seventies might disturb the digestion.

Theodore was thought to be 'strange' by his neighbours, but they would have approached him with some caution, if they had known that he was dabbling with De Lawrence magic.

He was a short, stocky man with a marked stoop and his left eye protruded and constantly rolled in its socket. He had been born with this handicap, it bringing with it much ridicule especially at school.

He had toiled on his land for many years, cultivating just enough to provide for his basic needs but now he seemed preoccupied with other things. He had a ramshackle shed in which he stored his tools and bits and bobs, but lately he was spending more time than usual behind its flimsy door, reading and 'messing about' with all sorts of strange 'stuff'.

This change had come about following an encounter with a passing stranger some months before. Theodore had dropped into the local bar, ordered his Red Stripe and was leaning against the counter eavesdropping on a conversation between the stranger and one of the locals. The visitor seemed out of place with the local regulars for he was dressed in a smart executive suit and sported highly polished black shoes. Something that his drinking companion had been complaining about caused him to laugh derisively and say out loud, "Man, you can't blame fate fi your misfortunes you know. You need to be wise."

He spoke with only a tinge of patois in his voice.

"Tings no so easy," was the response to the newcomer's criticism. "Wi poor an tings a go fram bad to wus."

"I use to tink like that, until someone tell me about De Lawrence."

The company fell quiet.

Fearful faces turned towards the source of such an outrageous remark and one drinker hastily walked out of the door, leaving behind the name that should not be spoken, along with his half empty glass.

The very mention of De Lawrence, that secret society of Obeah, instilled fear into many a superstitious mind. The company shuffled about in apparent embarrassment, but eventually the silence was broken by the newcomer, who rudely proclaimed, "Well gentlemen, I can see why you'll never make good of yourselves."

One would have expected an angry response to such humiliation, but one by one the customers began to sheepishly follow their mate into the street, leaving only Theodore and the stranger to eyeball each other across the bar.

The reference to De Lawrence had certainly touched a note of fear.

The stranger continued in a sarcastic tone, "What about you man? Are you not frightened as well?"

"No! Mi a no one a dem, so tell mi di story," replied Theodore.

"Would you like me to indeed?"

The outsider looked over to Mister Swaby with interest, smiled, then invited him to share a bottle of rum. Theodore never turned down the offer of a drink and it wasn't long before the two of them were tipsy and engrossed in conversation about the magic of De Lawrence. Theodore sat entranced, listening to a story that would lead him to study the power of this ancient Secret Society.

[1] "If wah yuh sey is true, mi wi like fe hear some more."

Before they parted, Theodore was given details of how to make contact with De Lawrence. Thanking his new friend, he wove his way home to spend a sleepless night writing the letter that was to change his life.

Two weeks later an envelope arrived at Mister Swaby's mail box down in the village. It contained volume one of simple magical formulae that he learned and practised in his shed. Many an hour Theodore browsed over the names of herbs and oils that had strange names, like oil of 'dead man's bones' and 'tun dem back'. He learned about the mischief that could be wrought by burying cursed eggs and three penny pieces in your garden. He learned about the power of grave dirt and how to use the blood of a black cat, a dried toad or the plumage of the John Crow bird. He learned about the Law of Relantum, a witchcraft from the old country, that told him how to steal hair or clothes fabric from an intended victim. Such items would then become part of a doll or carved image which were used to make the person suffer. For days and nights, often without stopping to eat, he would sweat over his book of magic.

His friends and neighbours began to feel concerned for his welfare, but when they approached him to express this anxiety, he brushed them off with, [2] "Unu mine unu bisnes," or some such words.

He was changing.

At one time he was quite well liked and would pass the day in small chat with any passer-by, but now he was becoming such a grumpy and often unpleasant recluse that he was ignored by the villagers. When he made rare excursions into his fields, he was often seen talking to himself and the local children began to throw rude remarks in his direction.

He was obviously not looking after himself.

He became so absorbed in his new interest, that he decided to write for volume two of the book of magic, only to be informed by De Lawrence that he should weigh the matter of going further with his studies with some thought. They advised that greater knowledge was accompanied by greater risk but he persisted, until eventually the more advanced instruction book arrived.

Did he want to become an Obeah man?

Whatever his intention, it became more and more an obsession.

Unfortunately, he became preoccupied with a section in the book that talked about gaining spiritual power by eating the raw hearts of freshly killed animals.

Each day he ate a chicken heart, but when the last chicken was denied its egg laying Theodore turned his attention to the yard rats and eventually he set out each night to deprive the local neighbourhood of its cats and dogs. Even his own goats and cow fell victim to the compulsion. No-one suspected him of such nefarious deeds, but then his wife went missing. Comments in the village that Mary had not been seen at the market recently started off the kind of rumours that can easily afflict such a tiny rural community. Mary had left home two months earlier, moving in with her aunt, following a row over Theodore's change of behaviour.

The gossip spread after Aunt Bib reported to the police that Mary had failed to return to her aunt's yard one night.

[3] "Mi go si Theodore bout it. Im cuss mi an drive mi out a im yard," she told the local constable who then decided to pay him a visit, but only received the same treatment.

As is usually the case, the juicy gossip eventually died down when the villagers found other scandals to preoccupy their time. Perhaps Mary had found a romantic liaison further a field?

ಆಞ್ಞ

Young Daniel Morgan lay in the thicket at the bottom of Theodore's field reading a book borrowed from school. He was engrossed in a tale about a green dragon when he was startled by a gruff voice:

"Whe yuh ave fi gi mi bwoy?"

Daniel jumped up in alarm, dropped the book, then ran a few steps from the scene and turned towards the cause of his rapidly beating heart. It was Wes, the local tramp and beggar.

[4] "Yuh fritten mi yuh noah sah a creep up pan mi. Go weh."

[5] "A ungry, mi ungry. Mi ongle waan piece a bread."

[6] "Well mi no hav nuttin. Weh yuh no go badda Mister Swaby."

Wes nodded, then shuffled away, muttering to himself.

Daniel returned to the depression that he had made in the ferns, picked up his book, then lay there watching old Wes shamble across the field. The boy was aware of the strange ways of Theodore and was curious to know how he would respond to a beggar. He saw Wes knock on the shed wall and Theodore appear at the door, apparently cussing at the interruption. They were too far away for any conversation to be heard but Daniel saw the open hand, so he knew that Wes was into his begging routine. To his surprise, he saw Theodore smile, shake his visitor's hand, then invite him in. It was a disappointment really, for Daniel had expected there to be a commotion, rude words and even a bit of violence so with a shrug of his shoulders he returned to his green dragon.

A few weeks later Daniel lay amongst his favoured under-growth absorbed in yet another tale, about pirates. Once again he was disturbed but this time by Theodore, who had noticed the boy's regular visits to the copse of trees and had quietly crept over to catch him.

[7] "Weh yuh a do pan mi lan?"

Theodore stood over the boy, his bulging eye rolling in its socket.

Daniel was up on his feet and ready to make a bolt for home but Theodore grabbed him firmly by the wrist and began to drag him towards the shed. Daniel squirmed to get away but no way could he break away from that vicelike grip, until, tripping over, he was dragged bodily over the rough ground. He screamed but no-one heard and eventually he was hauled over the threshold and found himself inside Theodore's secret hideaway. He was to find no comfort there, for he was met by a musty smell that did nothing to allay his mounting terror. It was gloomy but he could just about discern the unholy contents of the hut. All around the walls were shelves that were packed with glass containers and small boxes for various lotions and powders. A dead John Crow bird hung at the back of the door. Here a pickled lizard floated in preservative and there a dried frog looked down on Daniel's plight.

He realised that his predicament was taking a sinister turn for Theodore left him sprawled out on the floor, headed for his bench and picked up a large kitchen knife. No way was Daniel waiting to see what was for dinner and leaping to his feet, he threw open the shed door and took to his wings, Theodore's curses following him across the field. When he arrived at his yard, it was some time before he could calm himself to tell of his encounter with Maas Theo.

His father set out to investigate the matter, but he never came back. He hadn't arrived home before night fall, so mother went to the village to inform the local constabulary, who set off with all due haste to apprehend Mister Swaby.

They found him sitting calmly beside his hut, engrossed in cooking his supper. An open fire was laid under a Dutch pot, in which simmered a delicious looking stew.

Without any sign of concern, Theodore turned to the policemen and said calmly,

[8] "Evnin Sah! Unnu waan dinna?"

Their response was less cordial. They were now at the end of their patience, for they had received many complaints over the

"...and found himself inside Theodore's secret hideaway."

last few months that seemed to be linked to Mister Swaby. His wife had gone missing and so had a tramp, Daniel had reported an assault and now his father had not returned home. That was more than enough to warrant a less than gentle interrogation, so our aspiring Obeah man was dragged away to the station. At first he remained silent but a few expertly administered beatings started to loosen his tongue and gradually the whole horrific story began to unravel.

Whilst he languished in jail, fate delivered the final blow to Theodore's questionable career. The October rains came. Rains that were often heavy enough to wash away roads and even houses.

The body was found by a local farmer. He really couldn't have missed it, for the stench that drifted from Daniel's favourite copse of trees could be smelt clear across Mister Swaby's field. The farmer had an inkling of what was to come, for a sweet rancid bouquet hung in the air, reminding him of 'gone off' meat.

The smell changed as he drew closer to the woodland. Now it was stronger and more unpleasant. No longer a scent but an oppressive stench that tried to turn him away and prevent him tracking it down. He pinched his nose to experience a brief relief but his sense of disgust was soon to return as he was assaulted by a smell most foul.

There on the ground before him, washed from its resting place by the heavy rain, lay the putrefying remains of a naked man, his chest cut open and the heart ripped out. It must have been decomposing for some time, for it stank so bad that the farmer had to vomit before he could hurry off to the Police Station.

The evidence was unassailable for many heartless bodies were found buried in shallow graves and Jamaica's own serial killer was to stand trial.

The proceedings were soon over.

A short trial found Theodore Swaby guilty of murders most foul but right to the end he denied responsibility:

[9] "Yuh Hana, a de book of De Lawrence tell mi *fi* dweet."

The judge looked down over his steel rimmed spectacles and replied, "My book of the Law tells me that I *must* hang you."

So he did.

Doubting Thomas

Police Officer Thomas Alexander Gordon was proud to be a member of the local Constabulary and carried out his duties with great zeal. However, the local residents would say, that passion for his work often carried him beyond his authority.

He had the nickname of 'Sniffer,' because he was always sniffing out trouble and if he failed to pick up a scent, he would manufacture evidence to be sure that he had his fair share of criminals in his notebook. It was even rumoured that he saw nothing wrong in using physical persuasion to obtain a confession or two.

One good side effect of his fervour though, was that crime levels fell in his district and wrongdoers kept well clear. This produced a paradox, for the more successful he was as a crime stopper, the less cases he had to solve. Thomas found this most frustrating for he enjoyed the hunt, so much so that he had to resort to looking for trouble by following the children home from school to 'prevent them getting up to mischief'. He would give one the occasional clip around the ear, proclaiming, "Dat a fi nutten, so behave yusef or yuh wi get a gud lickin'."

One day Constable Gordon was walking down his beat in Cambridge, pausing now and then to pry into this place and peep into that, when he saw an Obeah man, known locally as Kush, walking towards him. Kush offered a friendly greeting,

"Gud mawnin' afisa."

Thomas' only reply was to put on a well practised posture, legs apart, bent at the knees, and hands made into fists resting on his hips. Looking down his nose with disdain at Kush he said, [1] "Yu no Obeah agins de law in Jamaica, so yuh a bruk de law an yuh wi get mi attensan one a dese days."

Kush shrugged his shoulders and walked on about his business unaware of the hassle that was soon to follow this chance encounter with the local Bobby.

Thomas continued on his round, ruminating on the steps that he could take now that he had a new 'criminal' on his action list. He was soon on the Obeah man's 'case'. He started to make weekly calls at Kush's yard just to make his presence felt, but it didn't take long for these visits really to become harassment. Walking all around the house he peeped in windows and made himself a general nuisance. He would stand at the gate after dark; he did nothing but just stand there, watching.

Kush soon realised that he was to be the target for Thomas' newly revived enthusiasm, so he asked his young son Josh to remove all the accoutrements of his trade, including his Book of Magic and hide them away whenever there were signs of the Constable nosing around, to prevent them being 'used in evidence.'

This was done and after they had been concealed some-where in the bush, Kush was ready to brazen things out with Constable Gordon.

[2] "Wah yuh a pesta mi fa? Wah yuh ope fi fine?"

Undeterred by this frontal attack, Constable Gordon replied with a sneer,

[3] "Mi know wah yuh up to wid yuh Obeah nansense an I a go put a stap to yu lickle game."

[4] "Yuh hav no right fi a badda mi dis way."

Such a remark only fuelled the officer's resolve to find some evidence that would incriminate Kush, so he found some pretext to take him to the police station, allowing one of his colleagues to steal away to search the Obeah man's house. Josh had hidden the evidence well, so nothing could be found.

More frustrated, Thomas increased his investigations and tormented his victim both day and night.

Kush was a patient man but he eventually gave Thomas a warning:

"If yuh no leave mi aloone mi a go Obeah yuh."

The Constable fell about with laughter but when he managed to compose himself, he chuckled,

[5] "Doan tink yuh can frighten mi wid yuh superstition nansense."

[6] "Superstition nansense yuh caal it? Well wi a go si bout dat."

As soon as he arrived home, Kush sent his son Josh to fetch certain items from the stash in the bush, which included a duppy that he had tricked into a bottle with Oil of Repellence. The boy was then sent on a mission to trap a mongoose and it wasn't long before the necessary items for his skulduggery were assembled. A candle was lit in his consultation room and his voice could soon be heard chanting an incantation here and a curse there, all surrounding the name of Thomas Alexander Gordon. Over and over, his deep resonant voice sang out as he pottered about with his strange collection of bits and bobs. On a small rough table that he used as an altar, a mongoose sat unusually still in its prison cage. On top of this pen stood a duppy bottle. A calabash bowl rested before them and one by one he placed items into this dried, hollowed-out shell, some small animal's teeth, the skull of a cat, various herbs, graveyard dirt, a lizard's tail and finally a good drop of Jamaican rum.

Now was the time for the Spell of Possession.

"Passe, passe duppy passe possie en Mongoose initiatum entrant."

A frightful wail came from the bottle and moments later the mongoose began to race around its prison, as though something was chasing him. Finally, it fell to the cage floor in a trance-like state, just laying there, limp and unresponsive.

It was possessed by the duppy.

Kush took it up and placed it gently on the altar, for it was now the time to send it off to wreak mischief on Constable Gordon.

"Frappai manta succai Mongoose, gungi mangai pedde Gordon, mangai pedde Gordon, mangie pedde Gordon."

The mongoose shuddered, then returned to its normal state of alertness, looked around the room, leapt to the floor and raced out of the house.

⋘⋙⋘⋙

Thomas Gordon had spent a pleasant evening in his local bar, sharing a few drinks and gossip with friends. It had been a good day for he had apprehended a cow thief, who was now spending his first night in the 'lock-up'. It had been some time since he had made such a good 'cop,' so he had treated himself to a few extra shots of rum. By the time he set out for his yard he was feeling very mellow. His wife Lydia had already retired and greeted him with her snoring, so as quietly as the drink allowed, he undressed, slipped between the sheets, settled down and was soon deep in sleep.

At three-o-clock after midnight, something brought him to a state of half awakening. A pain in his toe made him draw up his leg and exclaim, [7] "Wah a gwan?" but the effect of his rum drinking quickly pulled him back to sleep.

There it was again, a sharp pain in his toe. This time he sat upright with a curse, "Damn it. Wah dat?"

Something scuffled across the bedroom floor.

Thomas was now wide awake and left his bed in great haste, intent on catching the intruder but without success, for whoever was tormenting him evaded detection.

Thomas' chase ended on the veranda. The moon was full and everything was well lit but no movement betrayed the prowler, so he sat down on the top step to examine his painful foot. His right toe had been bitten and blood was freely flowing, so much so that it required bathing and dressing before he could grumble his way back bed.

Thomas' wife slept throughout the commotion, as if in a trance.

The following day his toe throbbed something terrible, so he swore to bring his abuser to justice. Little did he know that his troubles were just beginning.

It happened again that night and the next and the next and his feet were in a really bad state before the week was up, so much so that he was unable to turn in for duty.

Then the gossip started.

Triggered off by a few words dropped in the bar by Kush, the bush telegraph was telling how a duppy mongoose had been sent to torment the local policeman and, as was intended, this story soon came to the attention of Thomas.

Constable Gordon's response was predictable.

"Nansense!" he shouted "Mi naah believe ...." but his voice trailed off as he looked down at his bandaged foot. Having reconsidered, he murmured, "Nutten no go so. Nutten no go so?"

He was remembering Kush having said, "Superstition nansense yuh caal it? Well wi a go si bout dat."

Sometimes he would sit up to keep a night vigil in the hope of capturing the raider but it was too wily to be caught, seeming to know when he was awake. Each time he succumbed to his weariness his feet were mercilessly bitten, again and again.

After three weeks he was in such a mess that he was unable to leave the house, so he sent a message to the Obeah man, asking him to call.

The following day Thomas was sitting on the veranda, his poor feet resting on a pillow, when Kush sauntered up the lane, walked up the path and sat himself down on the veranda steps.

[8]"Yuh hav sinting yuh waan seh to mi?"

Thomas was slow to reply, knowing that he was about to humble himself, but eventually he managed to stammer out, "Kush, mi tink mi mus apolgise to yuh."

"It happened again that night..."

Kush was going to relish the police officer's humiliation, so with a hint of sarcasm he replied, "Wah fah, sah?"

[9] "Fi a fallah yuh up like dat."

Kush looked at the bloody bandages, gave Thomas a knowing look, then replied,

[10] "Mi tink di two a wi gaan too far. A time fi it done."

There was a moment of contemplative silence, then Kush slowly arose from the steps, climbed onto the veranda platform, sidled over to Thomas and stood before his adversary. Both men looked searchingly into each others eyes, then they both began to smile, a controlled smile at first but as the foolishness of their dispute dawned on each of them, they spontaneously burst into uncontrollable laughter and shook hands.

ෂ෭ඏ෭ආ

If you are ever passing through Cambridge and come across Police Officer Thomas Alexander Gordon, don't forget to ask him his opinion of Obeah magic.

He will reply with a sly smile, [11] "Dat a fi yuh fi ask an fi mi fi seh" and walk on his way.

Bell, Book and Candle

There's a folk tradition in Jamaica that takes place at funerals. It is believed that the duppy of the dear departed will endeavour to return to interfere with the family and that these ghosts are particularly attracted to the young. To prevent such a visitation, the children, preferably babies, are passed over the casket containing the corpse by relatives or friends, who recite the names of their children out loud.

This will hold the duppy in its coffin.

Omission of this ritual will also make the ghost a target for the Obeah practitioners, who seek to wield power over the spirit and use it for mischief against the chosen living.

The following tale illustrates the importance of preserving these old time customs.

附අ෯ශ෯ඌ

Father Sean Kilpatrick had been called to officiate at the burial of one Renny Brown, who had recently died at the town Infirmary, once known as the 'The Alms Houses'.

As he drove from the security of St. Paul of the Cross in Mandeville towards Royal Flat, he was sad and preoccupied at the thought of burying some soon to be forgotten soul in an unmarked grave, at the back of the building that housed them during their time of need and poverty.

His heavy heart was justified, for as he drove off the steep winding hill into the yard, he was greeted by an only too familiar sight.

A small group of fellow inmates and staff were gathered around a newly dug shallow trench that would soon devour the crude wooden box that stood on the ground.

Seeing the priest approaching, a member of staff bustled her way towards him.

"Good to see you Father. We're all ready for you".

With a nod of acknowledgement, the Reverend Father took his place beside the coffin and looking down on the late Renny Brown, his fears were confirmed.

No fancy burial this! No fine shroud for comfort; just a clean sheet in which to wrap the cold stiff remains. No stone sepulchre; not even a marker stone or wooden cross, but worst of all no relatives by the graveside to wish Renny a safe journey to his maker.

"How tragic!" thought Father Kilpatrick. "It's grievous to leave this world with no home and without loved ones to remember who you were; no friends or family to mourn your passing. Poor soul!"

The priest stood silently contemplating for a long time, unable to bring himself to commence the formal words of remembrance.

He had spent some twenty years looking after his flock in Jamaica and he knew his congregation well, being aware of the traditions and superstitions stemming from African roots, which surround their burial rites. He knew that, in spite of their staunch Catholic upbringing, many still believe that the dead hold great power and may return to haunt the living.

"Duppies they call them."

Speaking his thoughts out loud, he raised a few eyebrows amongst the tiny gathering but he was too preoccupied to notice the silent question.

How many times had he carried out his duties at funeral observing young children being passed over the body of the deceased as it lay in its coffin to keep its ghost at rest?

"I hope that Renny's spirit won't be persecuted by an Obeah man."

He stood for a few moments, checking out his thoughts.

"Goodness me, what am I saying? I'm a Catholic priest. Why am I thinking such nonsense?"

Shaking himself from his reverie, Father Kilpatrick began the Service for the Dead, much to the relief of the patient bystanders.

It was soon over.

The box was placed in the trench, then covered with red soil, leaving only a mound of dirt to remind folks that Maas Brown was now in his new residence. The final prayer was said, signs of the cross were made, handshakes closed the proceedings and the tiny congregation shuffled its way back inside for tea.

Father walked towards his car to begin his thoughtful journey back to the fellowship of the Rectory, but before he could reach it he was apprehended by an inmate who had evaded the shepherding of the attendants.

An old man with greying hair stood in his path. Bare footed and dressed in nothing but a smock, he took his stand, waving his arms in frantic fashion and fixing his wild eyes on the advancing cleric.

Father felt panic rising, but he smiled and greeted the man with a soothing, "Hello, my son. How can I help you?"

This provoked a loud howling and gyrating that caused the Lord's ordained to step back in alarm.

"Calmly now, calmly! Tell me what ails you brother."

The crazy dance ceased and with a pointing finger the dishevelled man advanced until he was in striking distance, then stopped, lowered his arm and with a surprisingly quiet and controlled voice, pleaded, "Elp 'im Fada! Di Obeah man a cum fi im duppy!"

"My Son, I don't believe in such nonsense."

This was not a well thought out remark and it set our inmate off into his frantic dance again.

"Mi seh, mi seh 'im cum tonite. No mek dem tek mi fren!" he shouted, and having accomplished his mission, the old man turned away and twirled across the yard to join his cronies.

Father Kilpatrick watched in silence, brooding on the prophesy and striving to draw some sanity from this strange encounter. He had lived amongst the Jamaican people long enough to know how fervently they believed in duppies, witchcraft and the like. He knew he had to respond to the wild man's plea. As unreasonable as it seemed, he really couldn't let things go unheeded.

ভ৪৩৪৩ন

That evening, after he had picked at his supper, the Right Reverend sat in his old armchair, preoccupied with the afternoon's events.

"What must I do? My reason screams that it's only superstitious nonsense, but what if...?"

This thought was enough to prompt him to lift himself from the safety of his chair and scuttle outside to pass under the connecting veranda that led into the church, through the large main door, down the aisle and into the vestry.

"Now what do I need? My travelling communion case might be of value."

He opened his trusty companion and ran his fingers across its contents. Everything was there: chalice and silver box containing the host, two small bottles, one containing wine and the other full of blessed water.

"These will be useful. Now what else I wonder? Must take a crucifix, a bell, a missal and a candle stick. Oh yes, a candle." To these he added a small statue of the Virgin and a rosary and loaded them into his car, then gathering his vestments, he set off once more towards Royal Flat.

Night was drawing in and with his mind so preoccupied with what might befall, it was more than one pothole in the road that obliged and punished him for his lack of concentration.

For the second time that day he slowly drove up the zigzagging road that told him that he was back. It was quite dark now, but as he negotiated the last corner, the car's beam of piercing headlight revealed the very person that he had hoped not to meet.

Beside the newly filled grave he could see a man dressed in black from head to foot, with head bowed as though in prayer and as the light struck his back, he slowly turned his head towards Father Kilpatrick, to reveal a countenance riddled with hatred. It was the Obeah man come to claim Renny Brown's duppy.

Threatening with shaking fists, he shouted,

[1] "Go weh! Yuh nuh hav no bisnes yah!"

The Reverend Father had stepped from his car, but he paused in the face of this onslaught and stood watching his enemy making invocation to whatever power was his master.

On the mound before him, the Obeah man had placed two lit candles in lanterns, one at the head and the other at the foot of the grave that cast a weird flickering glow on the proceedings. At his right side stood a glass bottle, in which he hoped to imprison Renny's duppy. At his left sat a calabash bowl containing animal bones, feathers, egg shells and human teeth collected from various grave robbing excursions. Standing proud in the centre of the grave stood a large bottle of dark Jamaica rum, intended to tempt the ghost to rise.

"By di Book of Makabee, mi demand yuh cum to mi!"

Making short jerky movements, the Obeah man seemed to grow in stature as he commanded Renny to return.

A most terrible cry rose up from the grave and the witch doctor smiled.

"Cum to mi, mi dear. Mi hav wuk fi yuh."

Father Kilpatrick could not bear to witness this wickedness and he let out a mighty cry.

"No! No! I won't let you commit this outrage!" and gathering all of his religious paraphernalia from the car, he rushed towards the ghastly ceremony.

The Obeah man spun around with a growl to face him and with his left palm facing his opposition he made a circular movement in the air.

Father Kilpatrick thought that he had run into a brick wall and some evil force slowly lifted him up, then cast him violently down onto the ground and held him by the throat until he was quite unable to make a sound. Turning back, the witch doctor began the ritual over, but as he focused on the task at hand his power over the priest waned enough for the Father to painfully rise to his feet, don his vestments, once again gather up the tools of his trade and run to the opposite end of the grave to face his foe. He kicked the candle lantern away and took up a defiant stance.

The Obeah man raised his left arm once again, but before he could recast the spell, Father Kilpatrick lifted the crucifix above his head and cried out, "In the name of Jesus of Nazareth, depart from this unhappy soul!"

The Obeah man folded his arms and grinned.

"So yuh a challenge mi. So be it den!" and with this remark the 'science' man drew a leather pouch from his pocket and undid the thong to reveal a fine dark powder. Pouring some into his palm, he blew it into the air towards the minister. It rose up, spreading to form a swirling cloud that slowly took on the form of a ghastly demon preparing to swoop down on the priest.

The Reverend Father cowered down, but quickly reaching for his bottle of Holy water, he released the stopper and cast the

"It rose up... [and] slowly took on the form of a ghastly demon..."

miracle water right into the face of this horrible monstrosity. Contorting with fear, the demon's face exploded into a rushing wind, leaving only the black powder behind, that settled all over the Obeah man, causing him to shiver from head to foot as his magic returned.

The bang drew frightened faces to the windows of the home that peered out into the darkness, looking for an explanation for the commotion. The sight of this duelling pair set usually silent voices into a clamour of alarm.

Now it was the turn of the church!

Out came the chalice to be placed on the grave mound and filled with Communion wine. Out came the silver box containing the wafers that represented the body of Christ. Out came the beautifully decorated stole, that was kissed with due reverence and placed around the priest's neck. Out came the Missal and Reverend Kilpatrick began the Mass.

The Obeah man didn't like this one bit and he took a few steps back from the grave with his palms over his ears to shut out the blessed words. As the Mass was said, a voice sounded from the coffin.

"Tank yuh Fada! Tank yuh Fada!"

On hearing this, the Obeah man responded with an angry roar,

"Enuf a dis. Mi cum fi Maas Renny duppy an nuttin a go stop mi!"

Bending down, he rummaged in his calabash and drew out a handful of his magical objects, which were cast down on the grave with a grand flourish. Speaking words from some ancient language, he picked up the rum bottle, removed the cap and poured some of the contents over the burial mound.

Everything was still, as though expecting the arrival of some malignant entity and our two combatants were both drawn into this menacing silence, until it was broken by a sound under the rum soaked earth.

The priest then bore witness to an event most horrible.

From below the surface of the grave came the sound of rending timber, the ground shuddered and a crack appeared to release a wrinkled hand that clawed its way into the moonlight to grasp at the now half empty bottle of rum.

The witch doctor yelled in triumph.

Father Kilpatrick felt himself about to weep, but gathering his composure he raised his Missal and ringing the bell he cried out in his best clerical voice, "Oh Father in Heaven, through the name of our Blessed Virgin Mary, grant our dear departed the power to drive away evil, so that his soul may be guarded from all the assaults of this Obeah man."

Massa Brown's hand became still and lifeless.

This fight between the church and Obeah magic went on and on throughout the night, each contestant gaining ground, then falling back in the face of each counter offensive. By dawn, both rivals had sunk to their knees from exhaustion, but they still fought on, striving to become the champion in this battle for the soul of Renny Brown.

CₒᴈᏚᏮᏎ

Unbeknown to each contender, the news of their title fight had spread around the district, for whilst their horns were locked in this seemingly endless contest, members of staff had slipped quietly away and taken news of the frightful event to surrounding homesteads and you know how the bush telegraph works in Jamaica. It didn't take long for the neighbourhood to become conversant with the odd happenings in Royal Flat. The gossip spread like a forest fire, reaching as far afield as Williamsfield, Clifton and Comfort. Folks were called from their slumbers and small groups assembled in the streets to shout and gesticulate. Many a suggestion was volunteered to save the poor soul. The men recommended taking up their cutlasses to deal with the matter head on, but it was the women who finally won the argument, submitting a solution of their own.

C3 EO EO CR

There had been a brief respite from the combat, for both gladiators were running out of rituals and spells and all that seemed left for them to do was to curse at each other.

As they knelt facing each other, an arrogant cockerel sounded its greeting to the dawn, then far off the sound of singing drift towards them. Far away and as yet indistinct, the music gradually formed to become a hymn, sung by many women. They came closer and closer until the words became discernible:

"It makes the wounded spirit whole,
And calms the troubled breast;
'Tis manna to the hungry soul,
And to the weary rest."

From all around, women came, carrying their babies and walking hand in hand with the young children. Up the winding road and into the institution's grounds, scores of them, all singing and wending their way to the grave side.

The Obeah man skulked back, for he knew what was afoot and that his work was thwarted.

Calling out its name, each child was lifted over the grave. One by one, on and on in a line that took a good fifteen minutes to pass, until the hand of Renny Brown, which was still protruding lifelessly out of the soil, twitched and opened wide. As the last name was called, it slowly slid back under the ground from whence it can and witnesses to this day claim to have heard a great sigh emit from the earth.

The battle was over.

Renny was at rest.

Obeah

That if you want a good report from your boss at work, all that you need to do is to place Obeah charms over the floor?

CR⊗SO⊗CR

That a Prime Minister of Guyana stated that Obeah practice should not be outlawed? He maintained that all cultures should be allowed their traditional rituals and practices, arguing that if the Christian Church can have its rituals and sprinkle Holy Water, then surely witch doctors may do similar.

CR⊗SO⊗CR

That the following are some of the articles used to make Obeah charms: rusty nails, the teeth and claws of a cat, bones, pins, feathers, snail shells, finger or toe nails, powdered glass, bird's nest and insects?

CR⊗SO⊗CR

That if you have just received a spell from an Obeah man or woman, you must go straight home? Do not stop, look back or speak to anyone. Do not get caught in the rain. Any of the afore mentioned may cancel the spell or turn it against you. (See the story – Never Look Back.)

 CʒꙄꙄꙅ

That frogs, with their mouths padlocked, were seen outside Law Courts? (See story – To Divert the Course of Justice.)

CʒꙄꙄꙅ

That it was common practice for farmers to have their crops 'dressed' by Obeah to prevent theft?

CʒꙄꙄꙅ

That Obeah men become Rollin' Calves when they die – so do murderers and butchers? (See author's book, Duppy Stories).

CʒꙄꙄꙅ

That one Obeah man of great notoriety, purported that during a two year period, he killed two hundred and forty one people and made a further six hundred and fifty five suffer?

CʒꙄꙄꙅ

That Obeah practitioners can give you 'big foot' (elephantiasis), cause you to lose your job, drive you from home or even kill you by 'magic'?

ೞೲ೪ೕ

That the liver of a human corpse, when ground with sugar is claimed to be Obeah poison?

ೞೲ೪ೕ

That Obeah men, who where slaves, swallowed their implements and brought their magic in their hair? This was why the hair was shaved before coming ashore.

The Reluctant Obeah Man

*P*apa sat on the veranda fingering through his Almanac, one foot on the top step, his other planted on the soil of the yard.

My father, William Anthony Plummer, affectionately known as Taata, was a self educated man who often sat with us to read from his Encyclopaedia and other books. However, it was the knowledge that he gleaned from the annual McDonald's Almanac that was responsible for the local community rumour that he was an Obeah man.

This grew just because he was well read, versed and successful in husbandry and he was happy to voice this knowledge at the village agriculture meetings and share it with his neighbours. He talked about the best times to plant crops and the best times to impregnate live stock. Skilled at 'reading' the weather, he would look up at the moon and say, "Leonie, di moon full a wata, rain soon cum!"

An intelligent man, his thirst for new methods made him use the latest innovations in 'grafting' plants and he became adept with herbal medicine, but this only added to his reputation of being a 'science' man. After all, his knowledge, to the ignorant, was seen as magic or that the devil was telling him all of these things. Mind you, that didn't stop these superstitious neighbours from coming to consult with him, but Papa never took money, for his advice was always freely given.

I remember one time, when an old lady came to him with a most unpleasant ulcer on her leg.

"Dis sore pon mi leg a get bad!"

Papa sat her down on our rocking chair and dressed it with a poultice made from a mixture of washing up blue, iodaforme, flour and egg white. Her gratitude resulted in her bringing culinary delights for weeks to come.

Things were no different at school.

Because Mama and Papa encouraged and tutored me at home, I always passed my exams in great style, but this brought me little joy in the community for I often heard women admonishing their children with,

[1] "Whe mek yuh cyan pass yuh exam, like Leon Plummert!"

[2] "But Mama," they would protest, "yu know a Obeah mek she pass. Har puppa a big Obeah man!"

Mind you, I rarely had any hassle from those kids, because they were too frightened of my father, but these beliefs sometimes had a sinister or amusing effect.

I remember one hot July, as I was playing jacks on the veranda, two men walked up the path towards the house.

"Good evlin miss. Does one Mister Plummer live 'ere?"

"Yes sa!"

I gave Papa a call and he came out from the living room.

[3] "A weh yuh want mi fah, gentlemen?"

The taller of the two strangers glanced in my direction and said quietly,

[4] "Well, di bisnis private sa!"

"Bib!" (That was the affectionate name he gave me). "Bib! Go play round di back, mi love."

With a nod and a smile, I skipped off the veranda and made as if to run around to the back, but the moment that I was out of sight I dropped to the ground to silently crawl into the gap between the floor and the red soil of the yard. Like a stalking Indian, I wriggled along until I was under the veranda floor, at a point that I knew so well.

My secret hiding place allowed me to hear all that transpired above and I could even see through a knot hole in the timber as my papa and the two strangers began their conversation.

Both of the visitors seemed restless and the one that had so far remained silent fidgeted about, then preceded by a nervous cough, he said, "It really 'at tidday!"

Papa gave him his special smile.

[5] "Mi sure yuh no cum fi taak 'bout di wedda. Weh yuh want mi fah?"

Gesturing to the porch bench, papa sat down on the rocking chair, lit up a home made cigar, smiled again and waited patiently for them to declare the purpose for the visit. Another tongue tied stillness followed, that was broken by the tall man.

"A nuh nuttin fi di Obeah man fi do!"

Papa raised his eyebrows and replied,

[6] "Nah ax mi nutten. Mi no noah nuttin bout Obeah!"

[7] "Ebrybady seh yuh a science man!"

I could see papa shaking his head but the stranger persisted with, [8] "Ef yuh dweet, mi wi pay yuh!"

[9] "Kip yuh moni kawz mi nuh waan it".

The visitors glanced at each other to exchange looks of mutual confusion but a response was forthcoming.

"Wi waan yuh fi urt smaddy!"

Papa looked ruffled, put down his cigar and looked to rise from his chair as he said,

"A fool ting dat yuh waan mi fi do man! Wha di man do yuh?"

The callers told a story of a boy who had made a member of their family pregnant against her will. They had reported the matter to the police, but they were told that nothing could be done. Suffering such injustice, they now sought revenge, giving out the boy's name and asking papa to kill him.

Papa was seemingly unmoved, then in that quiet voice of his, he said,

[10] "Gwan back a yuh yard. Mi wi si weh mi can do!"

As soon as they disappeared down the lane, he cried out for mama to tell her of this horrendous request made by the strangers.

Mama came out, carrying an orange bunch which she had been tying in the kitchen.

"Yuh mus waarn im!" she counselled after hearing the tale.

"Arite!"

I was told later that papa found the parents of the condemned man who lived in St. Catherine, 'up the hill' in the bush. His warning of the threat on their son's life was gratefully received and my father and this family became firm friends.

The boy was quickly sent away to a safe place. It appeared to the community that he had just vanished. Sometime later I heard that he had been sent to America. His sudden disappearance was interpreted by the felonious pair that papa had fulfilled their request to 'hit' the boy and dispose of the evidence.

We never heard from them again but to be safe we kept the story in the family.

ೞೲಬಿಂೞ

Papa's reputation as being an Obeah man dogged him all his life, but his disposition was such that he paid little heed to the gossip, although he would occasionally express how bemused he was to hear such superstitious nonsense. He did, however, have a great sense of humour and mischief, and these helped him to turn gossip around to work in his favour.

One such occasion concerned a bullfrog.

Papa once removed a piece of old post from the ground in our backyard. I can't recall what it had been there for but if papa said that it had to go, it had to go. It left behind a cavity that he never could be bothered to fill up. The hole sat under a coffee bush, which in turn was overshadowed by the outspread branches of a large mango tree. As the depression filled with rain water and damp leaves from the canopy of branches, it seemed that such a gloomy spot would not be an attractive home for any creature to take as its habitation but this cool dwelling place was soon taken over by a frog, a very large bull-frog, which seemed to be most pleased.

Well, he would have been pleased, if only he had been left alone, for it didn't take long for myself and the local children to find him and there's nothing better to torment than a 'spitting' bullfrog.

"...a miniature lasso that was carefully lowered..."

We would dance around, singing rhymes and poking the poor fellow with sticks to make him puff up and spit, until papa would shout from the veranda,

[11] "Stop dat! Im wi 'pit pon unu."

This was fair warning, because bull frog spit, that we called 'cocobay', would burn and sting, especially if it caught you in the eye.

One day, papa had a few of his cronies in the yard to play some dominoes. I was in my secret hiding place and I saw one of them looking towards the hole down the yard.

[12] "Wha di pickney dem a do anda yuh Caafi bush?"

[13] "Dem a tarment mi frog. Im caa tek it nuh mo'!"

His mates exchanged knowing glances and later when papa went indoors for some cold Red Stripe beer it was likely that they whispered amongst each other, saying,

[14] "Mi tell yu so! Taata a siance man. A di frog im use wen im a do im Obeah."

Well, it didn't take long for such silly gossip to spread around the area and come to the attention of a real Obeah man who lived close by. Papa later told me how these rumours were to lead to a laughable event that was talked about for months.

He said that one warm night he sat meditating on the veranda, when the stillness was interrupted by stealthy cracklings in the undergrowth near our mango tree. Papa put out his cigar so that its glow wouldn't reveal his presence in the darkness and he strained his eyes into the night to locate the intruder. At first nothing, but as his vision adjusted, he was able to home in on the prowler. A dark shape was crouching close by the spot where the bullfrog was settled down for the night.

Papa tiptoed down the veranda steps, preparing to rush out and seize the trespasser but before he could call on his adrenal glands to prepare him for the fight that might have followed, the moon broke free of the clouds and illuminated the whole scene.

There before him was a man he knew well, for the figure skulking in the darkness was the local Obeah man.

Papa dropped silently to his hands and knees and stilled his breath to remain undetected and watch the unfolding scene.

The Obeah man was peering into the frog hole and making quiet cooing noises, as though to soothe the uneasy tenant. He took some thin vine from his pocket and proceeded to make it into a miniature lasso that was carefully lowered over the frog. It took a number of attempts before the loop fell correctly into place, then gently it was raised, bringing the creature up to the lip of the hole. The Obeah man sneered in triumph, for he knew that father's powerful pet would soon be his, so he extended his free hand and drew closer to his prize.

SPLUUUUURT.

The frog had swelled like a bloated puffer fish and then it unleashed a foul stream of fluid full into the Obeah man's eyes. With a scream, he let go of the lasso and clawing at his face, he leapt to his feet and left papa's yard at considerable speed.

It was many months before papa could stop chuckling at the memory of this poor man running away from the frog, but unfortunately for him this episode did nothing to minimise his reputation as a man of magic.

His frog had bested the Obeah man and his notoriety once again spread throughout the district.

His denial was never accepted, so it was with great reluctance that he had lived with the title of Obeah man.

Long after his death and indeed to this very day, there are many who live in Porus, who will remember with great affection, my father, William Anthony Plummer... the reluctant Obeah man.

The Stubborn Duppies

There was once a man living in the Parish of St. Mary. I say living but in fact he was dying and he lay weak and forlorn in the back bedroom of his ramshackle old house in the District of Guy's Hill.

Jacob had not been visited by his relatives for some time and if it wasn't for a kindly neighbour he would undoubtedly already be in his grave. Known as Aunt Dor in the community, she would bring him cornmeal porridge in the morning, see that he was washed and presentable, then make him soup for his supper.

As he became weaker, however, he began to ramble on in a way that concerned her, for he was muttering something about a duppy.

1 "Whe mek im no lef mi alone, Aunt Dor?"

2 "Who yuh a tark 'bout?" she replied.

3 "Mi no noah a who, but im won't lef mi."

4 "Wha im a do?"

5 "Im seh bad tings 'bout mi, an dig mi inna mi ribs when mi a try fi sleep."

Aunt Dor found that it was of no avail to try to comfort him, for he was convinced that he had a regular visitor.

One evening, as she carried his soup onto the porch and approached the front door, she heard a terrible scream followed by fiendish laughter. Her first inclination was to run away, but her concern for the safety of Jacob drove her to rush into the house and through into the bedroom. He lay in bed, squealing and waving his arms at a dark figure that was laughing and leaning over him.

[6] "Mek im go weh, mek im go weh!" Jacob screamed.

Aunt Dor spoke in the most commanding voice that she could muster; [7] "Who or wha yuh be, yuh betta cum outa dis ouse now!"

The figure slowly turned around. It wore a black funerary suit and black shoes that must have been very smart when it was laid to rest, but now they were dirty and unkempt. Its face was covered in soil stains that ran down over sunken cheeks. Protruding eyes found Aunt Dor and a wide grin began to form on its face. The parting lips revealed blackening teeth and a mouth that released a smell so foul it caused Aunt Dor to step back in disgust. In a high-pitched voice, it said, "Sure mi dear, but mi wi cum back tomorra."

The figure shot out of the door, leaving a stench of rotting flesh in its wake.

The reality of the situation caught up with Aunt Dor and she sank to her knees in fright.

The following day she was having words with a Myal woman called Four-eyes because of her claimed ability to see and talk to 'spirits' of the dead. Such a woman would be just as much feared as the Obeah woman, for she was also credited with the ability to use these spirits to injure or kill the living. It was the Myal who claimed to be able to release the *shadows* of people who had been nailed to Cotton trees by Obeah practitioners.

Aunt Dor implored, "Mi 'ope yuh can 'elp Jacob."

Four-eyes replied, [8] "We wi cum tomorra an tek dis shadow fram yuh."

As promised, a group of the Myal congregation assembled outside of Jacob's house late the following evening. Dressed in white, wearing red and white bandannas and carrying bundles of twigs in their right hand, they formed a circle in the yard and began to dance and sing. Under the influence of good Jamaican rum, they were soon in a gyrating frenzy, twisting, dipping and lashing the ground with their makeshift brooms.

When sufficiently aroused, a group of them rushed into the house.

Aunt Dor stood wide-eyed and wrung her hands as the party clambered and banged its way from room to room.

Someone cried out,

[9] "Si 'im yah!"

Then another,

"Nooo, di shadow ober dere!"

Yet another shouted,

"Mi gat 'im. Mi gat 'im."

A woman cried out,

"Im get weh fram yah so."

This melee went on for a good half hour, until the raiding party tumbled back onto the veranda. They were all wet through with sweat and completely exhausted.

Aunt Dor ran over to Four-eyes and helped her to her feet.

[10] "It gaan. Yuh drive it weh?"

[11] "No!' replied the shaking Myal woman, "It too stubban! It no waan fi go weh."

When they had all recovered, the shamefaced congregation crept back to their homes, for not one of them could remember a previous occasion when they had been defeated by a duppy.

The duppy continued to torment poor Jacob, until Aunt Dor had to resort to visiting Shanti, the Obeah man, who said,

[12] "Whe yuh gu a Four yeyes fa? Yuh know dem naa gud."

In spite of this criticism, Aunt Dor pleaded with Shanti for help, until, for a fee, he agreed to catch the duppy in a small coffin shaped box. So armed with a bottle of rum, a phial of Oil of Repellence and his bag of magical charms hanging from his wrist, he entered the house.

What a commotion.

Shanti' s feet could be heard beating out a rhythm on the wooden floor and his voice chanted an appropriate incantation to draw the duppy into the coffin, using Oil of Repellence and a drop of rum bait.

[13] "Cum, mi fren! Cum rest inna dis lickle bax yah," cried the Obeah man.

[14] "Im mussa idiat. Whe mek im tink mi woulda do dat."

[15] "Si mi put some rum inna it fi yuh."

The duppy laughed,

"Mi woulda prefer Red Stripe."

So the argument waged back and forth, but it sounded unlikely that the duppy was going to succumb to Shanti's spells.

The witch doctor threatened, "Mi waan yuh, mi a go git yuh.'

"Do wha yuh waan fi do," the shadow replied.

It was a very angry Obeah man that stomped onto the veranda. "Aunt Dor, yuh wait yah. Mi a fi go a di cemitry. Mi soon cum back fi teach dis trouble maka mannas" and he marched off up the lane.

An owl hooted a greeting as he pushed open the squeaky cemetery gates.

Shanti looked up to reply, "Yes mi dear, yuh know wha go a 'appen," then purposefully made his way to a newly filled grave. He had brought a lantern which he placed on the shiny new sepulchre. This was soon joined by a bowl carved from the woody bottle-shaped fruit of the calabash tree. Taking the charm bag from his wrist, he took out a feather, an egg shell, a rusty nail, a pin, something that looked like a human fingernail and a selection of insects, which were duly placed in the bowl, to the accompaniment of words from some obscure language. Finally, liquid from the trusty bottle of rum was sprinkled liberally over the tomb and Shanti began the ceremony. Raising his arms to the moon he wailed, "Cum mi dear fren, mi hav wuk fi yuh." Stepping back, he crossed his arms across his chest, like some Egyptian mummy.

All was quiet and some five minutes later it seemed that his cry was all in vain, but suddenly there was a rushing wind and a mournful cry that echoed throughout the burial ground. Shanti had company, for a dishevelled man stood on the concrete sepulchre, waving his arms and shouting, "Wha yuh a do. Whe mek yuh wont leave mi in peace?"

"Mi hav wuk fi yuh."

"Mi no waant yuh wuk."

"No tell mi mi a go hav trouble wid yuh too," said Shanti.

He bent down to pick up a 'cow-cod' whip, which is made from the spinal cord of a cow; and when he raised it in his left hand, the duppy cowered in fear, for he was not keen to feel the stinging pain that it was about to inflict.

Thwack!

One blow was enough to send him running and it didn't take him long to arrive at Jacob's place, with Shanti chasing close behind.

Shanti yelled, [16] "Tek dis backle an mek di stubban duppy climb in de."

"Yes sah! Yes sah! but no lick mi again."

The duppy dashed into the house and started up a rumpus with the intruder.

Thump, bash, wallop! Someone was getting a good thrashing, but it wasn't until Shanti's new servant re-emerged, carrying the bottle, that the victor was identified.

"Im inna di backle, sah."

"Gud! Gimmi an go back a yuh yard."

"Tank yuh sah," and the duppy shuffled home.

The following day Aunt Dor and Shanti travelled to the north coast with their prisoner and somewhere near Salt Gut the bottle was thrown, as was the custom, into the sea.

The stubborn duppy never came back.

With the cessation of the torment, Jacob recovered from his strange illness.

If you are ever travelling through Guy' s Hill, don't hesitate to visit, for he likes nothing better than telling this story ... over and over again.

Maggoty, Maggoty

My maiden name is Leonie Louise Hibbert and I was born in Porus, in the parish of Manchester, Jamaica.

In 1957, when I was nearly nineteen, I emigrated to the British Isles to begin a new life as a trainee nurse, eventually returning to my native land to be with my mother in 1973, after my father had died the previous year.

I spent a short time at the old Mandeville Hospital but because of my qualifications as a midwife, I was soon posted to the Community Maternity Home in Malton, where I had a house built so that I could live close by.

Every day I ran a general clinic for the local community, which included educating on health issues, running a mother and baby clinic and providing dressing care for minor injuries. I was, in fact, a general factotum.

My tale really begins one morning when I met a local character, a tramp named Albert Powell.

Our paths crossed as I was walking my usual route to work. He was hobbling down the road in a really bad state, filthy from head to foot, his clothes looking as though they had not seen soap and water for some time. Something was wrong with his leg and he was obviously in pain.

"Good Morning Mister Powell. How are you this morning? Having trouble with your leg?"

"Mornin' Nurse. Yes Maam. Mi leg bad fi years, but nutten can get it betta, so mi haffi bear it."

"Why don't you pop into my clinic and I'll have a look at it for you?"

[1] "Ah Nurse. Eben if yuh luk pan it, it cyan get betta, a trick dem trick it nurse. A mi cross mi hav fi bear."

"You just come up. I would like to see it for myself."

With that last parting remark, I continued to the clinic and was greeted by a motley array of customers patiently waiting for treatment. It was a busy morning and by the time I was able to break for a well earned drink any thought of Mister Powell was furthest from my mind. My colleague and I had begun to clear up the inevitable mess of surgery, when who came walking in, leaning on his cane, but Albert.

"Mawnin' again nurse. Yuh aks mi fi call."

"Indeed I did Mister Powell. Come in, sit down and tell me about your bad leg."

[2] "Arite, but yuh cyaan elp mi. Mi hav dis leg sore fi a long time."

"How did it all start?" I asked, as I rested his leg on a stool and rolled up his trouser leg.

[3] "Well nurse, mi deh wid dis young woman many years ago. Di fambly dem no like mi, so dem Obeah mi. Trick mi leg."

I couldn't resist a little chuckle.

[4] "A true mi a tell yuh nurse. Dem trick mi foot an mi spen ebry quati a doctor, a Balm Yard, an nuttin elp. Wan Obeah man

tek aal mi moni an den seh im cyan elp, caus di trick too strang fi im."

I suppressed a smile as I examined his leg.

Somewhere, under the layers of filth, I found a dirty old bandage and dressing, which had been applied by some good Samaritan many weeks before.

Carefully unwinding the bandage, I found strips of gauze that had adhered to his skin. I soaked these and removed them with great care for fear that the tissue would come away and start up the wound all over again. My patience was rewarded. There was no evidence of an active ulcer for it had scabbed over.

"I'll have to clean up your leg to get a proper look at the problem."

"Anyting yuh seh nurse."

Washing his leg, I gently towelled it down, then to be sure that it was properly clean, I placed a bowl on the floor under the leg and poured hydrogen peroxide over the scab. Leaving Albert to 'soak', I went into the next room to fetch some clean dressings but I wasn't prepared for the sight that greeted my eyes on my return. I dropped the dressings and gave out a squeal that brought my colleague running to my side.

Albert sat quite composed and fascinated, looking at his leg.

[5] "Yuh si wha mi tell yuh nurse. Di Obeah man im trick mi leg wid magik dem."

The peroxide had loosened the scab, which had opened up to reveal a mass of wriggling maggots oozing from the wound and pouring down his leg, like lava pours from an active volcano. I had seen many sights in my time, but this certainly caught me

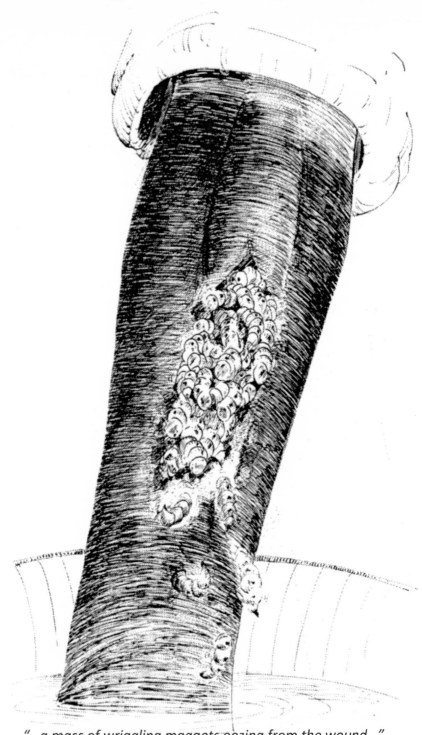

"...a mass of wriggling maggots oozing from the wound..."

unawares and I had to run away from such a revolting sight. Taking a moment to compose myself, I returned to the clinic room where my assistant was cleaning up the maggots that were trying to make their escape across the floor. Some even looked as if ready to fly.

Because they were not very keen to be disturbed, another regiment of the beastly things came marching out as I poured on more peroxide. I set to with tweezers and swab to lift them out of the ulcer, then applied disinfectant and redressed the crater.

We sent him away with instructions to report again the following day, which he did.

Another examination revealed more maggots. These were completely removed and his leg was redressed.

His vagrant situation was reported to the Health Officer but the doctor said that the best we could do for him was to get him into the Poor House at Royal Flat. Regular treatment enabled his ulcer to heal but Albert could not believe it.

Just before he left for the Poor House, Albert looked at me and said,

[6] "Nurse, mi go a all di doctor dem, Obeah men dem an lawd know who else, an nuttin no 'appen. Yuh a di ongle one fi elp mi an I a go tell ebrybody dat yuh a di best Obeah oman bout yah."

He must have done so because we had a sharp rise of business due to his recommendations, although there were those who would insist on calling me Obeah woman.

Old superstitions die hard.

Never Look Back

Two rich men lived not far from the Bamboo District of St. Ann, Jamaica.

It was clear that they were rich, because they rode fine horses and looked down on those less fortunate than themselves. Sitting high on a horse raises you above the mere donkey riders.

People in the district often wondered how Mike Ayres and Rupert Johnson always prospered. Every gamble they took seemed to be guaranteed success. One could say that they were lucky, or maybe God had given them both the gifts of the entrepreneur. Certainly every venture flourished but God had nothing to do with it, in fact the Almighty was likely to be concerned about the path these two rivals had chosen.

The reason for their success and prosperity was due to regular visits to the local Obeah man, but unbeknown to each of them they both called on the services of the same medicine man.

Wouldn't it have been nice if they had been partners, collaborating in common projects and sharing their financial successes?

Mike had been the first to pay a visit to a man known locally as Whangra.

[1] "Mister Whangra, sah. Tings naa go gud. Mi neba hav no moni. Wah yuh can do fi mi?"

"Tek a seat."

Whangra gestured towards a lonely looking stool placed in the centre of the bare board floor and when Mike was settled he stood behind and placed his hands firmly on his client's shoulders. They talked together for some time and Whangra plied him with questions to ascertain the true nature of his visit.

"So yuh tink mi can 'elp yuh?" the Obeah man queried.

"Some seh yuh can."

"But wah yuh seh, mi son?"

"Mi no noah sah, but yuh 'elp plenty people inna di villige."

"Arite, mi wi si wha mi can do."

Releasing his grip on his shoulders, Whangra picked up two lit lanterns and murmuring under his breath, began to walk around the chair. After three rotations, one was placed before Mike and the other behind. He then took a small looking glass, a large fan and a box of vials filled with different coloured liquids from his chest of drawers. The looking glass was ceremoniously placed on the floor between Mike's feet and spoken to in a formal manner.

[2] "Di glaas seh yuh fi paye."

Beads of sweat began to form on Mister Ayres' forehead and his voice cracked as he replied, "Ow much im want?"

"Anyting wi do."

So he obediently took some small change from his trousers and dropped the coins gingerly onto the glass.

Whangra picked up the fan and began to address it in the following fashion, [3] "Mi fren, if yuh naah cum outa di grave fi elp dissa poor man, it naah open, but if yuh a go elp im den show mi wan sign."

With a mighty crack that caused Mike to leap up in fright, the fan burst open in his hand and rushed around the room wriggling like a snake, dragging the 'science' man behind it. "Yuh si. Yuh si." Whangra shouted, but Mister Ayres was hiding in a corner, his eyes turned away from the 'miracle.' "It look like im a go elp."

There was no reply; Mike was too frightened.

All went quiet, so the Obeah man went over to the corner to lead him back to the chair.

Then came the vials. Each one was examined carefully, then three were selected and placed on the mirror. One at a time the stoppers were withdrawn and a few drops of the liquid were poured onto Mike's head.

[4] Mi 'noint yuh wid de ile a Success."

Then he took a second bottle.

[5] "Mi 'noint' yuh wid de ile a Moni."

Finally, he took up the Oil of Luck and repeated the ceremony. Following more words of council, Whangra took his fee, handed his customer the oils and led him to the door.

[6] "Mi a waan yuh befo yuh lef. Anybady a aask fi spell dem mus tek wah dem get, so yuh na tek dis a magic simple" and with that he shook his hand, nodded, smiled and said goodnight.

Mike seemed to be glad to get home and a hot drink of cerasee tea soon had him straightened out. He sat pondering on the experience well into the early hours of the morning.

Soon after his encounter with the Obeah man, a certain Rupert Johnson was to knock on the medicine man's door to receive the same services and soon after, both men began to prosper.

Their paths would cross from time to time, but love was not shared between them. A rivalry grew, for they sometimes vied for the same business and competed for the same contracts. Mike was fatalistic, seeing his rival as necessary to help him stay competitive, but Mister Johnson was not so charitable. He was jealous that Mike was equally successful. His envy was soon to turn into resentfulness and he began to take every opportunity to run down his fellow businessman. His bitterness became nothing more or less than old fashioned hatred and he schemed to damage Mike's business, but everything that he tried was to no avail. He was not aware that Mike was protected by the selfsame Obeah magic that had made his own business so successful, so he decided to go for another consultation with the witch doctor.

"Mi want yuh fi do someting fi mi Missa Whangra."

"Dem tell mi sey yuh a mek gud," he said.

"Yes sah, but me coulda do betta if mi couda get rid a Missa Ayres."

The Obeah man wasn't going to breach his professional confidentially by telling him that Mike was one of his customers, so he replied, "A who im?"

"Im a craas mi up sah, an mi want fi si im gaan."

Whangra could see that this rivalry might lead to an ongoing trade, because if it caused some problems for Mike, he would also be back asking for favours, so he was happy to offer advice to Mister Johnson.

"Ow bad yuh want fe si im go?" he queried. Rupert blurted out, "Mi want fi si im ded."

"Dat is a bad ting yu a ask."

"Mi wi paye yuh."

"Arite den. Yuh mus bury dis egg inna im yard."

"Fix it up fi mi den."

So he did and gave the following instuctions,

[7] "Do it wen di cack crow before daylite. Mek yuh wish, den lef an no luk back."

Whangra explained that to look back was very dangerous, as it risked drawing the curse back upon oneself. This warning was repeated a number of times, so that he would fully understand the consequence of frustrating the magic.

Whangra took his fee, shook his client's hand, nodded, smiled and said goodnight.

Two nights later Mister Johnson rode towards the yard of Mike Ayres on his mission to bury the egg and curse his rival. Dark clouds raced across the sky and nothing stirred in the bush beside the road. He furtively looked around for possible witnesses to his wicked mission, but everywhere seemed deserted.

There had been very heavy rain earlier, so folks were staying at home. When close by his destination, Rupert dismounted, led the horse a little way into the bush, tied it securely, then made the rest of the journey on foot.

All was quiet at Mister Ayres' house. No lights disturbed the darkness. Perhaps he was out or in bed. Checking the territory, Mister Johnson crept stealthily up the drive, looking for a suitable piece of land in which to bury the egg and finding one, he crouched, dug a small hole in the red earth and carefully planted his deadly curse.

A cock crowed to begin the early morning chorus.

He whispered, [8] "Mek Mike Ayres' life dun wid now."

Suddenly a dog barked at the rear of the house and this was followed by a cacophony of baying and yelping. His presence had been detected, so he leapt to his feet and rushed back to the road, the dogs yapping close behind.

The veranda lights came on and a weary house owner stepped out from the front door.

"W'appen?" said Mike, rubbing the bed from his eyes.

No-one replied, for by this time Rupert was hastily mounting Horse. Digging his heels deep into the flanks of the beast, he cried out to be taken away. Horse willingly responded, for the dogs were snapping at its heels. The pair left the scene with Rupert leaning forward over the neck of his animal like a professional jockey close to the winning post. They would soon be out of harm's way, away from detection by Mister Ayres and clear of the snapping yard dogs. Feeling that he had put a safe distance between himself and the house, Rupert reined back his mount and let him settle down to a steady trot.

All would have been well if Rupert had only remembered Whangra's warning about leaving 'without looking back.'

Twisting around on his saddle and raising himself up on the stirrups, he turned to look back down the lane, listening for any sign of pursuit.

"...looking for a suitable piece of land in which to bury the egg..."

At that moment the voice of Whangra seemed to resound from all directions in the bush, [9] "If yuh look back, yuh wi caal dung terrible curse pon yusef."

Horse shivered with alarm, rose on his hind legs, then bolted up the lane at full gallop. Rupert pulled hard on the reins, but to no avail. Horse was out of control and its rider was unable to retain his seat. With a fearful cry Rupert toppled from the saddle but as he fell he was unable to release his left foot from the stirrup and, howling in pain, Rupert was dragged along the rough surface of the road.

Then his trailing foot caught up in a tree root.

With a rending of flesh and a scream most horrendous, Rupert was literally torn up the middle, from his crotch to his rib cage. Horse hardly paused in his stride and Rupert's right leg was ripped from its joint to lay bleeding in the road, whilst the rest of his shattered torso continued with Horse on its blooded journey.

When the steed eventually calmed down, it slowed to a trot and came to a halt right outside the gate of Whangra.

The neighing of a horse drew the Obeah man out onto his veranda and there, at his front gate, was a sight most horrible.

He hurried down the path, to behold the battered carcass of Rupert Johnson which wasn't quite dead, so shaking his head and hissing his teeth, Whangra looked into the glazing eyes of his client and quietly said, [cviii]"Now yuh si wah yuh do. Mi tell yuh fi no luk bak."

Obeah

Did You Know?

That Obeah men attempt to capture the duppies of the recently deceased and imprison them in bottles? They place something in the bottle that the person was fond of in life, along with Oil of Repellence. This will draw the duppy to be trapped inside. Once captured, it can be used to wreak mischief.

If you wish to protect yourself from duppy attack, you must first prevent it rising from the coffin.

There are a number of ways to keep it in the grave:

1. Pass a child over the coffin during the funeral rites. (See story 'Bell, Book and Candle.)
2. If the deceased is a man, the wife must cut off her pubic hairs, put them in his hand and say, "There, you have what you want, now disturb me no more."
3. If you insert pins into the feet of the corpse, it will find it impossible to walk.
4. Duppies like to disturb you by throwing stones onto your roof at night, so if you cut out all of the pockets from its burial suit, it will have nothing in which to carry them.

5. The widow must tear her husband's handkerchief in half. Placing one half in his dead hand, she burns the other, so instead of tormenting her, he will spend his time looking for the missing piece.

(Such interesting death rites can be found in a fascinating publication entitled *Bush Doctor* by Sylvester Ayre; also published by LMH Publishing Limited.)

I wonder how you keep female duppies at bay?

೮ಶ೮೮೮೮

That when an Obeah man dies, things fly around his house, bumping and banging, creating a fearful rumpus?

೮ಶ೮೮೮೮

That there once lived an Obeah man named Amilkir, who was reputed to live in a foul smelling cave? He had some illness that prevented him from walking. Robbers, like 'Three-finger Jack' found his cave refuge from the law, so he 'worked' Obeah to prevent their capture.

೮ಶ೮೮೮೮

There are those referred to as Mial or Myal (Four-eyed). The people are rumoured to have the power to see and communicate with the dead. Like Obeah men, those with this gift carry miniature coffins in which to keep the shadows of poor unfortunates.

☙❦❧

That Obeahmen are often called Samfi men, which means that they are swindlers, cheats and tricksters.

☙❦❧

That if you're out and about at night in Jamaica, you may come across the groaning decapitated head of an Obeah man? (If anyone knows the history of the legend, I would, man.)

Come-Uppance

This tale is based upon an actual event that befell an Obeah man.

The racket could be heard all around the village.

Rupert and Joyce were at it again.

For weeks this common law couple had been having some differences and now Rupert's voice rose in anger. "Weh yuh a badda mi fa, woman?"

[1] "Fi eleben lang years mi lib wid yuh an al dat time yuh mess wid adder woman dem an it mus tap!"

"Which woman dem yuh talk 'bout? Yu eber si mi wid any a dem?"

[2] "If yuh no tap yuh go si wha a go 'appen!"

"Gwan den no. Cum out an go weh!"

"Arite den, a gaan, mi gaan den!"

Slamming the door behind her, Joyce stomped off up the lane to her mother, grumbling all the way about her 'ginnal' of a man and bantering back and forth with the local gossips, who had been standing on their porches with ears waggling to pick up some scandal.

Rupert came to the door and shouted after her, "Yu naa cum bak inna mi yard!"

More fuel for the news mongers.

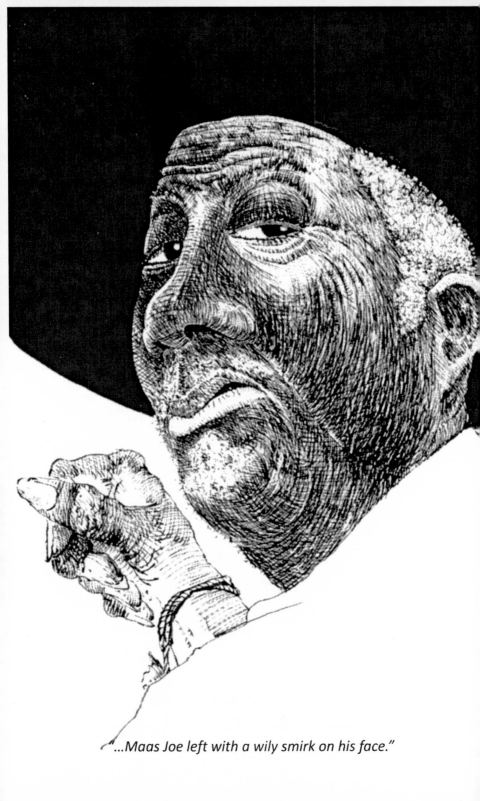

"...Maas Joe left with a wily smirk on his face."

The tiff was the main topic of gossip amongst the locals for many days and it soon came to the attention of the community Obeah man.

Such news of family breakdowns was his bread and butter, for he was skilled in manipulating family disputes for a profit. It wasn't long before he had made a plan to take money from the fractious couple.

There was something about him. He had a certain demeanour that demanded fear and respect but at the same time he was surrounded by an aura of cunning. As he approached Rupert's front door, his slow and deliberate step gave him the appearance of a prowling cat. Indeed, he had the most unusual feline green eyes and there were those who said that gazing into those small piercing orbs could turn ones hair grey. As always he carried a leather bag of *things* hanging from his bony wrist.

Rupert came to the door with a scowl on his face but the moment he saw his visitor his manner was quick to change. He was in fear of the 'science' man, so he quickly found a smile and an oily greeting, "Oh! A yuh Maas Joe! Wha mi can do fi yuh, Sah?"

The Obeah man replied in his usual smarmy manner, "Mi 'ear dat Joyce a give truble. Mi a wanda if yuh waan mi fi elp yu?"

Indeed he could, for Rupert knew that Mister Joseph Phillips had the power to bring her home and make her obedient, so he invited him in to discuss and make a formal agreement to place a spell on Joyce. The fee was paid and Maas Joe left with a wily smirk on his face.

The following day saw our witch doctor outside the house of Joyce's mother. Joyce was in the front yard and received him with some trepidation.

"Wha yuh want, Maas Joe?"

"Doan worri yusef. Mi jus cum fi waan yuh. Rupert a put duppy pan yuh to mek yuh obedient."

Placing her hands on hips and twisting her head she hissed, "Oh a so!"

"No get frighten mi dear," soothed Mister Phillips. "Mi can counter de magic fi a price."

Joyce, however, was not an idiot and she saw through the Obeah man's scheming ways, but she pretended to agree to receive Maas Joe the following day, when he would set up her bedroom for the treatment. She was told to bring a Bible, a red candle, a lantern, an exercise book and pencil, a large bowl, money and other illegal paraphernalia and he would come after dark.

I bet he would.

The moment he left, taking his knowing smile with him, she lifted her skirts and hurried to the local police station and made a plan with the officer to set a trap for the 'science' man. The policemen were to hide outside her house and listen out for her signal. When they heard her cry out, "Poor mi gal! Wha mi mamma neva si mi si now," they would know that she was ready for them to rush in and place the scoundrel under arrest.

So all was ready the following night. She had made the bed up clean, then placed a large bowl full of warm water to one side. Covering the dressing table with a hand embroidered runner, she arranged the Bible, lit the candle and the lantern, opened the exercise book and set the pencil ready just in time for the Obeah man's arrival.

Mother was asked to remain in the living room and the two of them went into the private place.

The local bobbies saw their chance to creep up to the house and hide just inside the door.

Inside the bedroom, Joyce was sitting on the bed, whilst Maas Joe was standing by the dressing table fingering through the Bible and muttering strange foreign words. Without turning around, he spoke to Joyce, "Tek aff yuh shoes. Mi waan wash yuh foot."

Joyce did as bid and the Obeah man wrote something in the exercise book, then gave her the Bible so that she could be reading a scripture out loud as he commenced the ritual of bathing her feet. He shook his head in a troubled way, seemed to pass into a trance and spoke in tongues but eventually said, "A duppy a sleep an eat wid yuh. Yuh know Miss Joyce, dis case serious." Rubbing her feet dry with a towel he continued, "Yes Ma, very serious. Yuh betta put all a yu moni pan di table, den tek off all yuh close an mi mek yuh a bath."

Joyce went along with his request. Placing the money beside the candle, she took off her dress, but speaking up loudly for all to hear, "Poor mi gal! Wha mi mamma neva si mi si now!"

In that instant the policemen gave a yell and rushed into the bedroom and after a brief scuffle Joe Phillips, the Obeah man, was carted away to the lockup, bemoaning his fate and shouting raucous remarks about the treachery of women.

Joyce made her way home to confront her husband.

"De Obeah man seh yuh waant mi fi obedient. Mi a go show yuh obedience" and without more ado she laid a cane across his back. All around the house, all through the yard and into the road, she wielded her stick to give him a good licking until his cries brought forth a crowd of jeering women.

His shame ensured that his womanising took a back seat for many months to come.

Tricks Of The Trade

The following are two brief accounts of how Obeah may be performed:

1. An Obeah man lived near a man who owned a lot of cows.

   He was covetous, so he approached a stranger to help him. During the night a phial of blue coloured water was buried in the farmer's yard.

   The farmer obliged him but as he stood, cup in hand, the stranger pretended to shiver and shake.

   [1] "Smaddy obeah yuh," he said and began to dance and wail around the yard, until he came to the spot where the phial was hidden.

   "Dig yah so," he said to the farmer.

   Digging, of course, revealed the curse, so the farmer sent for the Obeah man to lift the hex.

   The Obeah man obliged and it cost the farmer a cow.

   I can do that !

୧୫୨୨୫୦୧

2. A man was being disturbed in his sleep, by what he believed was a duppy walking on his roof.

    He sent for the Obeah man to drive it away.

    Climbing up on the roof, the 'science' man discovered that the branch of a tree was blowing in the wind and scratching on the zinc.

    He came down to report that [2] "Yuh 'ave one duppy a live inna yuh tree but no worry, mi can run im out."

    He took up a cutlass, climbed back up and lopped off the branch and threw it to the ground.

    [3] "Yuh naa go 'ave no more trouble now."

    The man paid his fee and was happy.

    Easy isn't it!

    All that you need is a believer.

The Rivals

Evelyn says that her mother told her this story.

My mother told me of an aunt, who used to run a business in the Old Market Square in Newmarket, St. Elizabeth, selling 'shave' ice, ice cream, patties, cakes and those kind of things. Another higgler had a stall close by, selling the same, so the competition between them was fierce and there was animosity between them every day.

Mother suspected that the woman went to see a local Obeah man, for the events that followed had all the signs of magic.

One Sunday, auntie cooked a nice dinner and everything was just fine. The dishes were laid out on the table with fry chicken and rice and peas, vegetables and everything. The family took their places at the table and a blessing was asked for the food and it was time to eat, so the lids were lifted on the serving dishes. Everything went silent, then a member of the family screamed for the dishes were full of maggots.

How did the Obeah man do that?

The contents of the tureens were hastily thrown out onto the yard, but when auntie went straight down to sweep up, she found the chicken, rice and peas and vegetables, everything, but *NO* maggots.

Now tell me, how did the Obeah man do that?

Then the problem spread to her stall, for the next day, when her first customer asked for ice cream, the lid was lifted to reveal a tub full of maggots. The Obeah man had no way of getting to her produce before she opened that morning.

So how did he do that?

The problem continued for some time, until auntie decided to see her own 'science' man. It didn't take long before retaliation was heading towards the rival woman, whose husband had a false eye that started to be found amongst the patties.

Every day she returned it to her husband, but the next morning, there it was resting amongst the patties.

I'd still like to know how that was done?

Auntie said she was a Christian, but she still continued with Obeah mischief and eventually her rival sold up and went away.

She prospered and went to America, where she got her stay and started up a restaurant, but eventually things did so well that she needed someone to work for her. However, instead of employing people over there, she brought family members as illegal immigrants from Jamaica. She was laying the foundation for trouble, because she employed her Obeah man to make false documents and fix up the paper work with magic, so that they would pass by American immigration without being caught. All of these shady pursuits were successful in the beginning, for business flourished and her family passed back and forth without any difficulty.

Her girls, however, were up to mischief and unbeknown to auntie, were about to bring her heartache. It is the way of

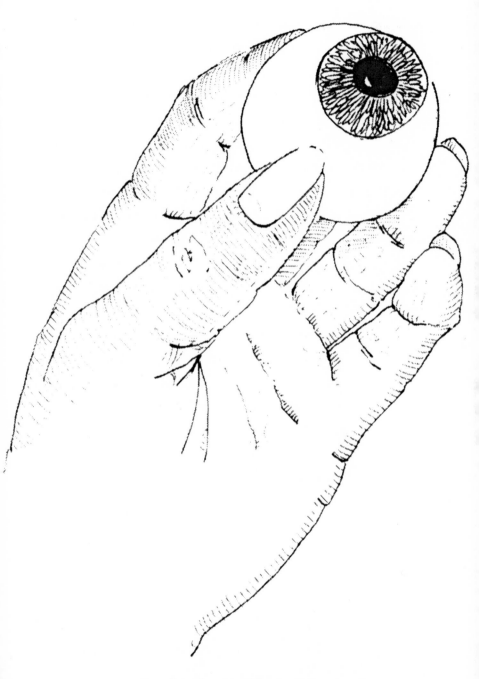

"...whose husband had a false eye..."

Obeah, that if you practice evil, then evil you will receive. Auntie was not aware that family members were not the friends she thought them to be.

The beginning of trouble was when two of her daughters came back from a visit home, bringing Obeah mischief with them. In New York, one was stopped in customs to have her suitcase checked but as the lid was opened a snake slithered out, fell to the floor and vanished amongst the hurly-burly of the airport. This caused quite a panic and the daughter was fined for bringing in unauthorised livestock.

The other daughter had *something* in her suitcase. *It* was released when she reached her mother's house. Then the trouble started. It later transpired that someone in the family was in debt to the Obeah man and he had sent this *whatever* as a warning.

Two weeks later, the eldest daughter was arrested in possession of cannabis, but she blamed her auntie, who she falsely accused of peddling drugs in the restaurant. Auntie called on the Obeah but she was still arrested. She lost the business and was deported back to Jamaica with all of her family.

Who was it that said that wickedness prospers?

To Divert The Course Of Justice

My name is Gene Francis and along with my friend, Earl White, I was to stand trial for the theft and butchery of a neighbour's goat, the evidence for our crime having been found in Earl's kitchen.

The court hearing was but a few days away and we both knew that we were likely to be facing some time in jail, for this was not our first offence.

[1] "Tings nu luk gud!" I said, as we both sat out on Earl's veranda. "Di police dem seh dem a go get wi."

Earl brooded for a moment, then grumbled, [2] "A cayliss wi cayliss. Mi a idiat!"

"Yes! Wi cyaan win di police dem."

"Wi can yuh know," Earl responded with a crafty smile.

I had not failed to notice the expression and was quick to question with, "Wha yuh a tink man?"

As he turned towards me, Earl's gold tooth flashed in the moonlight.

"Mi know a gud Obeah man who wi get wi out a dis yah mess."

The man in question was a Vernal Roberts, who was known by all to be a jeweller by day and, by some, to be an Obeah man

117

"...he kept an effigy of a black red eyed cat..."

after dark. In this way he tried to conceal the illegal activities that he carried out at home. People came from all over to visit the dark room in which he kept an effigy of a black red eyed cat that supposedly cured their ailments or improved their luck. Everyone had a fear of this animal that was covered and hidden under a black cloth in the daytime. Vernal called it Gygo and nobody dared to look directly into its red eyes but they were still drawn to its spell and the promise of some magical reversal of bad luck.

So the following night we knocked, with some apprehension on the door of Mister Roberts in Jones Penn. We presented our troubles to the Obeah man, who merely smiled and nodded his head from time to time. We had a warm enough welcome but still felt anxious as Vernal led us into the dark room and invited us to sit before the cat. Gygo was on a chest of drawers, surrounded by bottles, vials and two large crystal balls which were dimly illuminated by a single flickering candle that caused the red cat eyes to gleam as though alive.

Mister Roberts stood before his cat and chanted in a way that didn't make me feel any more at ease. Then he gave us some words of comfort, [3] "Uno jus do wah mi seh an uno wi arite pon di day." So we were sent away to buy rum and a bottle of Florida water, to return to the 'surgery' with them the following evening.

"Gud" said Vernal "Mek wi si now wat fi do." The rum and Florida water were presented to Gygo, then some foul smelling concoction was tightly tied into one corner of our handkerchiefs.

[4] "Tek di 'kerchief dem wen yu go a court. Wet dem wid Florida wata, an use dem fi wipe yu face, den cum si mi afta."

With that we were sent on our way, but he kept the rum.

છ૪૭૬૭ભ

Earl and I responded to the call of the police official and shambled from the waiting room of Sutton Street Courthouse, to take our places before Judge Reynolds and the case began.

A barrister for the prosecution stood before the court and began to argue his case. It was good, well-prepared and he had reliable witnesses. The evidence submitted by the police was unassailable, so when it was the turn of the young inexperienced lawyer who had been assigned to represent us, he stood to make his case for the defence, but he was soon floundering.

Things didn't look bright for us and our innings were going to be short, for Judge Reynolds was getting restless to sum up for the jury.

The instructions of the Obeah man had been for us to constantly wipe our faces, but in the midst of such anxiety provoking surroundings we had both forgotten. Earl suddenly nudged me: "Wipe yu face, man."

I was startled for a moment, but soon responded to his reminder. Slowly pulling out my handkerchief, I poured on some Florida water to wipe my sweating brow.

Earl nodded with approval and followed suit.

"What are you two doing?"

Our antics had not failed to come to the attention of the Judge.

⁵ "Nutten yur Ana! A 'at, it 'at in yah sah."

Peering over the top of his steel rimmed spectacles, Judge Reynolds waved his hand to the Court Bailiff,

"Bring those things to me!"

As bidden, the official collected the cloths from us to place them on the Judge's bench. One was tentatively picked up with a finger and thumb and carefully scrutinised. The repugnant odour from the concoction tied in the handkerchief drifted to his nostrils, causing him to turn away, wrinkling up his nose in horror.

Judge Reynolds seemed to know what he was holding and with a strangled cry he dropped the article, then quickly rose to his feet. Spectators in the public gallery saw that he was agitated and fearful, so they knew that something was seriously amiss when the Judge swept from the courtroom crying in a loud voice, "This case is adjourned until after the weekend!"

ଓଞ୍ଚଞ୍ଚ

"Gud gentlemen" Vernal Roberts patiently sat listening as we gleefully told of the effect of his magic on the Judge. "Yu mus go back a court, a mi wi do di res."

It was going to be a hot day.

We retraced our footsteps down North Parade the following Monday to be greeted by some sort of commotion outside of the main entrance to the courthouse. We mingled with, and listened to a small group of passers-by who milled about at the edge of the curb away from the foot of the steps.

One cried out, "Mi a tell yu a magic."

Another one said, [6] "A warnin' smaddy a gi."

Earl strolled over to the throng.

[7] "A wah kin a niz unu a mek so?"

A woman took him by the arm and pointing with a shaking hand, she wailed, "Luk pan dat."

A yellow powder resembling sulphur was sprinkled all over the walkway in front of the steps, across the threshold of the door and plastered on the lintel. Then another strange sight greeted us, for a John Crow bird, with a red ribbon tied around its neck was strutting up and down on the steps in front of the entrance to the Courts. More astonishing was the sight of an enormous bullfrog that sat on the top step staring at the crowd, its pop-eyes fixed and glistening. Bullfrogs are common in Jamaica, but not one like this, for its lips were fastened together with a padlock, someone having pierced the flesh and inserted the U shaped bar to allow only a muffled croak from the poor creature.

"Lawd, im mout seal up," I shouted.

Earl turned to me, "A wah dis mean?" he asked.

"A Vernal!" I replied.

As they prattled on, the circle of curious, frightened spectators failed to notice the approach of various employees of the court.

The prosecution barrister was first to push his way impatiently through the gathering, obviously in haste to get to chambers.

His eagerness soon came to an end, however, when he came face to face with the silenced frog. He fell back onto the circle of fidgety bystanders.

"What devil's work is this?" he stuttered and breaking through, he ran around to make his way to the back door.

Soon to appear was Judge Reynolds, who showed his con-sternation by bellowing something derogatory at the frog as he charged up the steps into the building, clearly most upset by the situation.

Other officials chose a variety of footwork to avoid their fear but the Obeah work was clearly making its mark. Jurors too, had to suffer the trial of getting pass these objects of magic, point-ing and whispering as they went.

Eventually we, the accused, made our way to the waiting room, chatting in good humour until the court reconvened. When our time came to present ourselves before the Judge, we found the court in an uproar. The morning's experience was being discussed with such agitation that Judge Reynolds had to beat his gavel with some vehemence before he could introduce enough order for the trial to begin again. When called upon to summarise the prosecution's case, the barrister seemed to be reluctant to say that his facts were unassailable, but instead introduced such phrases as, "We cannot really be sure ..." and "Who knows whether ..." which, of course gave our defence council a wonderful opening through which to launch an attack on the case of his learned colleague.

Judge Reynolds allowed many points of order to pass by unchallenged and was clearly not on good form in controlling the proceedings. He seemed to be in the same agitated state that had overwhelmed him as he left the court the previous Friday. His summing up of the case was quite a disgrace, for he made a biased plea to the jury that they make sure that the defendants be given every opportunity, by their realising that in law, "these men are innocent until proven guilty." He said this quite unnecessarily over and over again.

In many ways the trial became an absolute shambles and the press had a great opportunity to take liberties with their reporting.

The jury retired and returned with undue haste, seemingly so restless that the Judge had to settle them down.

"Members of the jury, have you considered your verdict?"

"Indeed we have your Honour."

The foreman of the jury rose slowly from his seat and looked furtively around a hushed court.

"We find the defendants ..." At that very moment both doors of the courthouse flew open with a mighty crash and Judge Reynolds rose to his feet and turned to face the intrusion.

Nothing was there but from far down the corridor we all heard the wet flip-flopping of something coming nearer and nearer.

I'm sure that I was not the only one present who shook a little when a large padlock free bullfrog came into view, entered the courtroom, hopped across to the bench and with an enormous jump dropped right on the Judge's head.

What a sight.

Our poor Judge was transfixed, unable to move even the smallest muscle. His eyes bulged from his head to match those of his new companion and his trousers seemed to be gathering water.

Nothing and no-one moved for what seemed to be an eternity until with a vibrating scream, the foreman of the court finished his sentence, "... *not guilty* your Honour."

Someone cried out, "Case dismissed" and set off a stampede for the exits. Moments later the courthouse was empty, empty apart from Earl, myself and Judge Reynolds, who still stood in terror listening to the frog, who's newly found voice resounded around the courthouse.

Earl and I stepped down from the dock, walked across to the bench, touched our foreheads to the honourable Judge and left him there to ponder.

Earl then turned away and headed for the exit.

As he turned into the main corridor, he looked over his shoulder and said, [8] "Cum Gene. Mek wi go tief anedda goat."

An English Obeah Story

A community of Jamaicans live in Catford, a district in London, situated south of the river Thames.

It is here, on Rushey Green, that the Rising Sun Bar is run by a likeable Jamaican and his attractive wife and the local black community gathers to drink and gossip.

One balmy afternoon in July, a group of men were sitting around a table on the decking that made an outdoor area near the main door. Empty bottles of Jamaican stout and half full glasses of lager littered the table for they had been in noisy discussion for some time. They had appraised the state of the British economy, criticised Blair, Bush and affairs in Iraq and bemoaned the lack of respect shown by the younger generation of today. They had, in fact, solved all of Britain's problems in no time at all. They then turned their attention to the homeland to rate the current performance of the West Indies cricket team, to lament the current fall in value of the Jamaican dollar and to debate the pros and cons of Patterson's government policies.

"Tings no gud back a yard, but mi miss it yuh si."

The heated debate ceased.

Wesley's remark had touched on homesickness and after a quiet pause they began to reminisce about good times back in the old country.

"Mama's gone now, but mi tink 'bout her a lot," said George.

Weston quickly changed the subject with a tale of school mischief and it triggered off noisy laughter as they shared the happy times when they were young. Tales of strict schoolteachers, of rolling in the bush with some plump girlfriend, of strolling, cutlass in hand, to cut a juicy fruit from a mango tree, of noisy games of dominoes outside the local bar and downing the occasional tot of white rum.

[1] "Wah yuh miss mose, Wesley? said Ivor.

[2] "Di wedda," was the reply "mi cyaan get use to di cole."

Weston gazed into his drink, then quietly replied, "Mi miss mi fambly back 'ome."

James laughed.

"Mi miss a gud game a domino wid di bwoy dem."

"Yuh can get dat yah too."

"A no di same," James replied.

There was a pause. They knew what he meant.

"Yuh rite, James. A no di same. No a no di same at all."

This observation came from Dean, who had not said much for most of the afternoon. He sat, can in hand, leaning back on the surround rail, his feet resting on the table, taking in the conversation.

"No!" he continued. "Mi miss all sart a tings. Mi neva cum a England till mi well over forty. Mi miss lots a tings."

James spurred him on with, "Like wat so?"

Dean removed his feet from the table, leaned forward, looked around the group, then declared, [3] "Uno know wah mi mean. Yuh know 'ow tings slow. A miss di 'soon cum'. I miss di patois. Dem call mi foreign wen mi go 'ome laas year 'cos mi hav English twang.'

Wes laughed and said, "Dat 'appen to mi too."

Dean nodded, then continued, [4] "Di frenliness a di people dem an de 'nosiness'. Mi love it man. Wi cyaan walk in a smaddy 'ouse fi food an gossip like back a yard. Wi a cum jus like di British dem. Wi haffi mek people know when we a cum si dem. Eben di food no hav no tase, fah it no fresh like back 'ome. Mi love mi aringe straight aaf a di tree." This subject was finding its mark. The men had become strangely quiet as personal memories began to rise.

A shrewd smile preceded Dean's next remark:

"Mi eben miss mi Obeah man fi im advice."

The ensuing shocked silence was almost visible.

James frowned. Weston raised his eyebrows. Ivor tutted his teeth. Wesley suppressed a nervous cough. George made as though to leave.

Dean had used the taboo word that was guaranteed to bring any conversation to a halt or prompt remarks like, "Wah dat yuh seh. Wi no taak bout dem tings ova yah." Weston broke the disturbed silence by blurting out, "Wat yuh mean yuh *miss* yuh Obeah man?"

Dean's smile was now a wide grin.

[5] "Wat unu a try fi seh, unu neba go to wah Obeah man."

Another silence followed.

Dean continued, [6] "Mi no hav no fait ina dacta, becaas a wan Obeah woman gi mi bush an it clear up wan problem mi did hav wid mi manhood."

Nobody supported Dean's enthusiasm.

In the weeks that followed, there was never an occasion when the boys gathered at The Sun for a drink and gossip that the subject of Obeah didn't raise its head and eventually Dean proposed, "It woulda nice if wi hav wi own Obeah man fi serve wi community."

George blurted out, [7] "Yuh mussa daff, weh yuh eva 'ear such a ting?"

"Mi," said Weston, "Mi 'ear 'bout wan Obeah woman in Nottingham."

"Mek wi try den. Wi can advertise inna di Gleaner" said Dean.

George left in a hurry.

Ivor said, "A weh yuh say man, yuh a talk nonsense."

From the ensuing remarks it was clear that Dean was alone with his wish for a community 'science' man, but undeterred, he decided to go it alone . Three weeks later the following advert appeared in a Jamaican newspaper:

An experienced Obeah practitioner is required to pursue healing work in London, England. A location for a surgery will be provided and a small wage will be paid until established.

Two weeks later he received a reply:

'Dear Mister Hylton,

I have just read your advertisement in the Gleaner. My name is Madam Kerada and I have been practising Obeah here in St. Thomas for many years. I have been considering joining members of my family in London, so your notice in the press is most opportune. I never dreamed of being able to continue with my profession over there and I hope that we will be able to make mutually agreeable arrangement.'

Dean began to correspond with Miss Kerada to glean more information, but it did not take long for him to be satisfied with her credentials and by the following January she was on her way to England, having made arrangements to stay with her children.

Dean offered her his parlour at his home on the Brownhill Road and all went quite well, for as Dean spread the news of her arrival Jamaicans started to turn up for 'treatment'. Slowly at first, but as her reputation spread, hardly a day went by that clients didn't bring their problems and ailments and waited in the hall outside the parlour. Even a furtive white face or two was seen taking their turn for her advice.

None of Dean's mates at the Rising Sun would come near and they were always ready to jeer at and criticise their friend's venture when he turned up for his drink.

George was especially scathing with remarks like, [8] "Mi no know wha yuh si inna dis Devil nansense."

[9] "No matta a wah, it wuk man."

[10] "Gweh. It naah wuk pan a boil inna mi behine," said George.

"Well! Madam Kerada 'ave a lot a people a go to her an swear dat she is gud. Not only dat, she wi give yuh gud luck as well."

"Yuh a idiat."

"Wait an si man."

The following month Dean won three million pounds on the Lottery.

"...having made arrangements to stay with her children."

Obeah

Did You Know?

That if something was stolen on the plantation, everyone was assembled in the graveyard and a coffin would be opened?

The priest would take up earth and place a small amount in each person's mouth. The thief's belly would swell and they would die.

ᘓᘔᘓᘔ

That it was a common superstition that, if you took it for granted, Obeah magic can take away your good health?

To this day, if you ask someone how they are keeping, they will rarely reply, "Very well, thank you." More likely they will say, "Not too bad" or "Could be better."

ᘓᘔᘓᘔ

That burning the Whangra plant was another means of obtaining a confession from a thief?

Boil it in a pot over a fire of leaves, then cut the root into four pieces. Give three pieces a Christian name, then bury them at the plantation gate and burn the fourth.

If the stolen item is not returned, the thief will break out into sores. (You will need to know the incantation.)

ৎৠৣৠ

If a farmer wishes to scare off thieves, he must kill a rat, then hang it up to attract John Crow birds?

John Crow is considered to be an omen of death under the control of Obeah men and will be enough to discourage trespassers on your land.

ৎৠৣৠ

That it is believed that Obeah men are able to catch a person's shadow? But fortunately there is also a ceremony to get it back. The victim must be dressed in white, with a white handkerchief on their head and taken to a Cotton Wood tree.

To pacify the duppies who live in the tree, they must be given an offering of eggs, chickens and cooked food. Those attending must sing and dance (Myal) as they parade around the tree, then wringing the necks of the fowls, the carcasses, along with the eggs, are thrown at the tree. A white bowl of water is placed before the tree and further singing will draw the shadow to the water. Everyone lifts up the victim and rushes him home and a white cloth is immediately applied to his or her head and the shadow made welcome.

ৎৠৣৠ

That Obeah men use 'tricks' to rob people, like placing baked coconut over a likely client's door to attract rats? They will then offer their services to 'Obeah' them away. Taking away the coconut, he sets poison and the job is done. One such customer failed to pay the bill, so a length of bamboo, stuffed with dead frogs, was inserted into her thatched roof to attract John Crow birds, who then damaged her property.

The Obeah man said that if she paid double, he would drive them away.

We all know how he got them to go, don't we now!

𝚌𝚛𝚎𝚘𝚜𝚘𝚌𝚛

That if you find a three-penny piece in your yard it has been planted to bring you harm? To test whether it is from an enemy, put lime on it. If it foams, you're safe from the Obeah. (Mind you, if you bring a silver coin to lime, it will always foam ... it is its nature!)

Cock On A Stick

The influence that Obeah can wield over some people is often more to do with their own limited education and superstitious nature, than any actual power of magic. This story was an actual experience of my wife, when she worked as a Public Health Nurse in the Mile Gully area in the parish of Manchester, Jamaica.

I was most anxious for the welfare of Dora Spencer. Dora came, from time to time, to the mother and baby clinic for general advice and check-ups but my concern was that, each time she came, she was carrying a new baby. She had delivered some nine children and it looked as though this was only a beginning.

"Dora," I would say to her, "You really must do something about your fertile ways. You can't carry on like this."

[1] "A mi 'usban' nurse, im naa leave mi aloone. Anyow, mi mus hav out mi lot."

There is a belief amongst some Jamaican women who live in deep rural areas, that they carry their 'lot' from God in the womb and if these babies are not presented to the world, sickness or even death will follow.

"Well, you're showing signs that you're overdoing things and I would like you to consider using some kind of birth control."

[2] "Mi wi si wah mi 'usban' seh nurse."

Carrying her newest baby in her arms and leading another child by the hand, she made her way home. That was likely to be the last time I saw her until she came to report that she was pregnant again but only two weeks passed before she came shuffling into the clinic. "Mi tell mi 'usban' nurse an im seh mi mus go to de Obeah man."

I smiled and said, "Oh yes and what did *he* have to say?"

"Im seh mi mus cum back to yu."

"Well, there you are then, you've come back to the right place."

[3] "Mi eben talk to Albert. Im seh yu get im ulcer foot better an yu a gud Obeah woman."

What could I say?

"So your husband will agree to planning your family's future?"

"Mi tink so nurse."

"Alright then Dora, I'll give you a regular supply of condoms to take to your husband."

[4] "A rubba dem nurse?"

"Indeed they are, Dora."

[5] "Mi 'usban' neva use dem before, so im naa go know ow fi use dem."

There is reluctance amongst many Jamaican men to use condoms or 'boots, coats, jackets or rubbers' as they call them, preferring the sensation of 'skin to skin'.

I assured her, "You needn't fret, I'll show you how to do it."

Then I looked around the clinic to find something to represent a penis and finally came across a long handled sweeping brush.

"Here we are Dora. Just the thing, Now imagine that the broom handle is your husband ready to enter you."

Her attention became well and truly focused on the broom as I waved it before her eyes.

"Now all that you have to do is remove the rubber from the packet, like this. Then squeeze the air out of the nipple with finger and thumb and place it on the end."

With that, I gently rolled the condom down the handle and then gave Dora the opportunity to practise the same simple procedure. All went well and Dora went home with her supply of condoms to add this to her role as a dutiful wife.

I didn't see her for many months, but one day as I was carrying out house calls around Comfort Hall, remembering that Dora lived close by, I decided to pay her and the children a visit. Driving my Beetle into her yard, I scattered the dogs and chickens and parked. Moments later I was surrounded by a horde of clamouring children who swarmed all over my trusty old transport.

"Mamma, it's nurse," they cried.

Dora appeared on her veranda and it was obvious that she was pregnant yet again.

"Oh, Dora, what have you been up to?"

She stepped down and shuffled towards me, eyes seeking the floor, as though hoping to find some object that might divert her embarrassment.

"De magic neva wok wid mi nurse."

"Really? That's strange."

"Mi do de same ting yuh seh nurse."

She beckoned to me to follow her onto the veranda, through the living room and into the bedroom. There she bent down to retrieve something from under the bed.

"...I scattered the dogs and chickens..."

It was a long handled broom.

[6] "Si nurse," she said with pride, "same way yuh show mi fi put it pan di broom tik."

I couldn't help laughing.

Covering the end of the handle ... was a condom.

The Will

Old man McPherson had been ill for a long time and it came as no shock to the family when he passed away in his sleep.

His boys were not happy about having to perform last offices, so they were relieved when a good neighbour's wife came over and offered to wash him, lay him out and place burning coffee and herbs under the bed to preserve the body.

With their mother gone to her grave the preceding year, the sons had to make all of the funeral arrangements. The younger son, Roy, was aware that there would be plenty of money in the will to share with his brother, but he had always been of a mean disposition and was soon suggesting to Ezra that they make no fuss.

"Mek it simple fi save moni," he said.

Ezra was having none of this, for his father was well respected in the district and he knew that friends and family would be expecting the celebration of 'nine-nights' to be something special. To the annoyance of Roy, Ezra made sure that the local community were made welcome to visit, as was the custom.

During the first two days and nights the house was open for friends and even strangers to call. They sat around, eating, drinking and sharing memories about the life of the deceased, but

Roy spent most of the time muttering to himself about the unnecessary expense.

On the third day, Mr. McPherson was interred in a sepulchre at the bottom of the front yard. All went well and folks came from all over the parish to wail and sing their farewells. Ezra spent the next six days preparing for the 'ninth' night, the time set aside for the final celebration of father's life. It was the custom for there to be a party of splendid proportions and in spite of Roy's protests, Ezra said, [1] "Papa weh gud to wi, so mi a gi im waan gud sen aaf."

So it was that the company was greeted by a veritable banquet of curried goat, fried fish, ackee and salt fish, rice and peas, dumplings and a plentiful supply of alcoholic beverages. Roy, ever resentful, found himself quite unable to join in the festivities, for he still brooded over the extravagance laid out before him. It did not prevent him, however, from filling his plate, taking off to a corner and tucking into the banquet.

The gathered folks sang and chatted through the night and it was very late before the well fed and tipsy guests began to drift away.

The following Tuesday the brothers made their way in best suits, shirts, ties and well polished shoes towards Baynes, Roberts and Whylie Solicitors, to a meeting arranged to read the will.

Mister Roberts was waiting for them. He gestured them towards two seats placed before his desk.

"Come in gentlemen and take a seat".

"Tank yuh sah."

The office gave an impression of utter chaos. Every available space was covered by impressive looking leather bound books and documents tied together with ribbons. The only place free of this clutter was a small round table near the window, on which resided a silver tray and an expensive looking decanter, half filled with sherry-coloured liquid. Two cut glass tumblers kept them company. An unkempt looking Mister Roberts shambled around the desk to park himself in a leather chair that looked as though it had belonged to his grandfather.

"Now then, gentlemen, what can I do for you?"

With a look of surprise, Ezra said, "Wi cum fi hear papa will sah."

"Ah! yes."

Mister Roberts began to shuffle amongst the many documents piled up on his desk and, after what seemed to be a fruitless search, he gave an affirmative grunt and drew out the relevant file.

"Now let's see."

He sat for ages perusing the document, until the boys must have wondered if he was about to fall asleep. Finally, with a sudden cough he leaned forward, spread the will on top of the crowded desk, looked over his spectacles and smiled at his clients.

"The wishes of your father are quite straightforward. He has left everything to you good gentlemen."

The boys smiled at each other, then Roy said, "A wah wi expek sah."

"Maybe so young man but your father has asked me to convey his wishes as to how the estate is to be divided."

Roy was adamant as he quickly said, "Wi expek fi get 'alf each sah."

Mister Roberts sat back, pushed his glasses to the bridge of his nose, then quietly said, "Not so, young man!"

Roy stood up and blurted out, "Wha dat yuh say sah?"

Waving Roy back to his seat, the solicitor took up the will and began to read out loud, "...It is my wish that my son, Ezra Herbert McPherson, being my firstborn, shall receive the major portion of my inheritance. This is to include the house and the ten acres of land upon which it stands. Any money that survives me will be divided as follows: Three quarters will go to my son Ezra and ..."

The proceedings came to a halt as Roy, leaping to his feet, shouted and swore his disapproval of his father's judgement.

Mister Roberts was visibly shocked by such disrespectful behaviour, but Ezra merely intertwined his fingers and silently looked at his knees. He was not at all surprised to hear his father's wishes, for he knew how mindful papa had been of Roy's slovenly ways and how he had always performed his duties around the farm in a slipshod manner.

An indignant Mister Roberts said in a surprisingly quiet voice, "I really must ask you to leave my office, Mister McPherson."

Roy obliged by stamping his way to the door, wrenching it open and slamming it as he left.

When Ezra arrived home that day, it was to find his brother pacing about in the yard, demanding that all manner of curses and plagues be showered down on father, Ezra and the solicitor. He would not be pacified and he rushed off in a tantrum. To

Ezra's utter amazement, when Roy did return late that night, he sauntered into the yard with a great grin on his face, as if nothing untoward had happened. Ezra would really have been concerned, however, if he had been made aware of Roy's whereabouts during the absence.

After leaving his yard Roy had made straightway for his local bar to make himself thoroughly unpleasant to the barman and get drunk, but Fred, the proprietor, had much experience in dealing with this sort of behaviour. Many a soul came to drink away the problems that they were having at home and over the years Fred had become skilful in soothing such customers and putting their money in his money box.

Two hours passed and Roy's temper subsided, to be replaced by a more mellow mood and, as his blood alcohol level rose, the reason for his displeasure gradually unfolded to Fred.

"Why yu no go si Mister Thompson an aks im fi im advice?"

"Mi neva tink 'bout dat. A waan gud idea doah."

So saying, Roy slipped from the stool and made his way to Mister Thompson's Obeah surgery.

"Mi want yuh fi move mi bredda."

With a touch of sarcasm in his voice Mister Thompson said "Wah yuh mean *move*. You mean yuh want mi fi run im 'way?"

"No!" replied Roy, "Mi mean kill im."

"Mi wi do it, but it wi cost yuh moni an waan duppy fi 'elp mi."

"Mi wi do anyting."

"Arite, if yuh sure, go 'ome, den meet mi a di graveyard tonight. Carry a bottle a rum an one dead chicken."

Roy paid the fee and made his way to his yard in a much better mood. After all he would soon be well off.

That night, when Ezra was asleep, Roy sat up on his bed and listened for signs of activity in the house. When he retired, he had stretched out, fully clothed, to be ready for the night meeting that would bring mischief to his brother. Nothing stirred, so he gingerly tiptoed to the bedroom door and out into the passageway, pass his brother's bedroom, through the lounge and into the yard.

It was no problem carrying the bottle of rum but the capture of a fowl from the chicken house without causing a ruction was a different matter. Putting down the bottle, Roy crept into the shed and stood for a moment to acclimatise his eyes. Three hens sat on a perch before him, ruffling their feathers in response to his intrusion but making no sound. Roy did not move, giving them time to settle again, then with great precision he quickly grasped head and beak of the nearest bird with his right hand and before it could flap its wings, enveloped it with his left arm. A quick twist of its neck and the bird was dead. It was over in one silent moment and Roy slunk off into the night.

It had been easy so far but the scary part was yet to come.

When he left his yard the moon was full, but as he approached the cemetery, storm clouds began to fill the sky. Distant thunder and a rising wind began to set the scene for impending acts of wickedness.

Roy tiptoed between the graves calling out quietly, "Anybody deh yah?"

A response from his left led him to Mister Thompson, who stood amongst a cluster of white sepulchres, his back turned towards a giant of a cotton wood tree. He was dressed all in black, unsmiling and quite still. He spoke with a low sigh, "Yuh bring de tings dem."

Roy shivered and his voice tried to desert him, "Yes sah!"

"Gi mi dem."

Roy was unable to respond, so Mister Thompson advanced on him in a way that could only be described as *flowing* over the ground.

Roy gasped.

"Wah yuh a do bwoy? Gi mi dem!"

Grasping the offerings, the Obeah man turned to the tree and threw the chicken at it and with a mighty shout, cried, "Cum fren, somebady waant fi si yuh."

Then taking a generous swig of the rum, he spat it out over the white trunk of the duppy tree and said again, "Cum fren, mi hav somebady yah fi si yuh."

All was silent. Roy trembled and sweat formed on his brow.

Nothing happened and he sighed with relief, but suddenly a sound, a sound of movement like leaves being disturbed behind him.

He was transfixed to the spot, not daring to twitch a muscle but there it was, that rustling again. It took strength of will but he slowly turned around. What a relief, there was nothing to be seen, nothing at all, but as he was about to return his attention to the ritual behind him, a flash of lightning momentarily lit up the ground. There before him lying between two white tombs, was a motionless figure dressed in what looked like a white funeral shroud.

"...and raced pell-mell from the scene..."

Then a peal of thunder woke the corpse.

With a fearful wail, the body rose up and cried out, "A who waant fi si mi?"

Roy had no intention of answering, for he leapt high in the air and raced pell-mell from the scene, straight for the cemetery gates and away up the road, just like a greyhound.

Mister Thompson stood with hands on hips, laughing up-roariously, then turning to the corpse that now stood beside him, said, "Gud!"

The 'body' threw back the muslin from his head and replied "Well! Yuh shudda si im face sah."

This 'corpse' was the Obeah man's assistant, who had been instructed to lie in wait to surprise Roy.

It is said that Roy never returned to his yard.

Conclusion

Our journey has ended and hopefully we are all in tact. You were indeed courageous enough to read these stories, many of which are authenticated tales about the activities of Obeah practitioners, but the question I ask is, 'How convinced are you that the power of Obeah magic is *real?'*

The stories about poisoning are well documented in court cases over the last two hundred years but evidence for being able to capture duppies in bottles and using them to cause mischief is another matter.

Do you really believe that you will die if you walk under a rusty nail tied over your porch, or that our shadows can be captured and nailed to trees? Are you persuaded that grave yard dirt thrown on your roof will bring trouble to your household, or that if you are out late at night you may meet a screaming skull?

All cultures have their fears and superstitions.

Don't walk under ladders. Don't let a black cat cross your path. If you want something to happen you must keep your finger's crossed and so it goes on and on, one old wives' tale after another.

I am a sceptic, but one thing that I have learned is that strong beliefs can *hold* great power *over* us. Our superstitions can *make* consequences come to pass, so that it seems that we create the reality that we deserve.

I am sure that an Obeah man understands what I mean and knows how to use this concept for his own ends.

Notes

The Medallion

1   "I want the two of them dead."

2   "Ah, the Obeah man."

3   "I am going to see the Obeah man to see if he can help me."

4   "Who is that?"

5   "What do you want? What have you come for?"

6   "Do you know what you're asking? Do you know what you're asking me to do?"

7   "It's serious you know."

8   "Yes, I know, but you will get money when my house is sold."

9   "Papa! Nathaniel! Where are you?"

10   "I went home this morning and my brother and father weren't there. I've looked everywhere, but I can't find them. Father can't walk, so what's happened? I'm baffled."

Rattle, Rattle

1   "Who's throwing something on my roof?"

2   "If I ever catch you, you'll see what I'll do to you."

3   "Somebody is trying to 'obeah' me, but I don't care how much he tries, he can't succeed."

4   "Every night I hear stones being thrown on my roof and I don't like it."

5   "Ghosts know how they should scare, but I have the cure for that."

6   "Put this in your wallet. Be careful that you don't lose it and everything will be alright. My fee is five hundred dollars, please."

7   "What ! Not again?"

8   "Who's that banging on my door and making so much noise?"

9   "It's me! Bertha Johnson! I have a bone to pick with you. I've paid a lot of money for you to work for me, but nothing's happened."

10   "Do not bother me, woman. Do you know what time it is?"

11   "I begged you to give me a hand with my problem."

12   "Oh! It's you miss. It upsets me when somebody makes such a noise on my door and I don't know whom."

13   "The magic must be too strong. You will need special magic from me!"

14   "Sprinkle this around your house and nothing will come close. Five hundred dollars is my fee."

15   "The obeah man cannot help me. I will have to catch the wicked spirit."

16   "I want you to hide in the bush next to the yard and catch anybody who is making mischief and beat him."

17   "Obeah man! Obeah man! What are you doing here?"

De Lawrence Fire

1   "How are you doing Esmie? You must be lonely!"

2   "Oh Aunty. I am managing but I miss Lester!"

3   "I see. You know that you can come to see me at anytime."

4   "I am getting used to my little flat, and I am managing, but thank you!"

5   "Alright! But don't forget where I live now."

6   "Even though things are bad back in Jamaica, I'm home sick. If I could only afford the flight."

7   "We would like to help, Esmie. Do you want to go to De Lawrence. It would help you."

8   "Oh, you mean obeah. Why didn't I think of that?"

9   "I will contact them if you want"

10   "Lord my God! What is this!"

Power Over The Mind

1   "Not bad thanks, but I don't like how somebody ripped me off."

2   "Somebody broke into your house? I wonder who?"

3   "I have my suspicions, but if they think they'll get away with it they are making a sad mistake."

4   "Police! Why would I tell the police? I am going to the Obeah man."

Get To The Heart of The Matter

1   "If what you say is true, I would like to hear more."

2   "Mind your own business."

3   "I went to see Theodore about it. He cursed me and drove me out of his yard."

4   "You frightened me you know sir, creeping up on me. Go away."

5   "I'm hungry. I only want a piece of bread."

6   "Well, I've nothing. Why don't you go and bother Mr. Swaby?"

7   "What are you doing on my land?"

8   "Evening sir! Would you like dinner?"

9   "Your Honour, the book of De Lawrence made me do it."

Doubting Thomas

1   "You know that Obeah is against the law in Jamaica, so you've broken the law and you'll have my attention one of these days.

2   "What are you pestering me for? What are you hoping to find?"

3   "I know what you're up to with your Obeah nonsense and I'm going to put a stop to your little game."

4   "You've no right to bother me this way."

5   "Don't think you can frighten me with your superstition nonsense."

6   "Superstition nonsense you call it? Well, we'll see about that."

7   What's going on?"

8   "You have something you want to say to me?"

9   "For following you about like that."

10 "I think that we've both gone too far. It's time to finish it."

11 "That's for you to ask and for me to say."

Bell, Book and Candle

1   "Go away! You have no business here!"

The Reluctant Obeah Man

1   "Why can't you pass your exam like Leonie Plummer!"

2   "But Mama,... you know its Obeah that made her pass. Her father is a big Obeah man!"

3   "What do you want me for, gentlemen?"

4   "Well, its private business sir!"

5   "I'm sure you didn't come to talk about the weather. What do you want me for?"

6   "Do not ask me anything. I do not know anything about Obeah!"

7   "Everybody says you're a Obeah man!"

8   "If you do it, I will pay you."

9   "Keep your money because I don't want it."

10 "Go back home. I will see what I can do!"

11 "Stop that! It will spit on you."

12 "What are the children doing under your Coffee bush?"

13   "They are tormenting the frog. It can't tolerate it any more."

14   "I told you so! Taata is an Obeah man. He uses the frog when he does his Obeah."

The Stubborn Duppies

1   "Why doesn't he leave me alone?"

2   "Who are you talking about?"

3   "I don't know who he is, but he won't leave me alone."

4   "What does he do?"

5   "He says bad things about me and digs me in the ribs when I try to sleep."

6   "Make him go away."

7   "Whoever or whatever you are, you'd better leave this house now!"

8   "We will come tomorrow and take this shadow from you."

9   "See him here."

10   "Is it gone? Did you drive it away?"

11   "No! It is too stubborn. It doesn't want to leave."

12   "Why did you go to Four Eyes? You know they are not good."

13   "Come my friend! Come rest inside this little box here."

14   "He must be an idiot. Why does he think I would do that?"

15   "See, I put some rum in it for you."

16   "Take this bottle and make the stubborn 'duppy' climb in it."

Maggoty, Maggoty

1   "Ah nurse. Even if you look at it, it can't get better. It's been 'obeah-ed'. It's the cross I have to bear."

2   "Alright, but you can't help me. I've had this ulcer for a long time."

3   "Well nurse, I got involved with this young woman many years ago. The family didn't like me, so they 'obeah-ed' me. They tricked my leg."

4   "It's true I tell you nurse, they 'obeah-ed' my leg and I spent every penny I had on doctors and Balm Yard (a form of healing), but nothing helped. One Obeah man took my money, then said he couldn't help, because the spell was too strong for him."

5   "You see what I tell you nurse. The Obeah man has cursed my leg with maggots."

6   "Nurse, I've been to all the doctors, Obeah men and Lord knows who else, but nothing happened. You're the only one to help me and I'm going to tell everybody that you're the best Obeah woman around here."

Never Look Back

1   "Mister Whangra, sir, things are not going well. I never have any money. What can you do for me?"

2   "The glass says you must pay."

3   "My friend, if you won't come out of the grave to help this poor man, don't open, but if you're going to help him, show me a sign."

4   "I anoint you with the Oil of Success."

5   "I anoint you with Oil of Money."

6   "I'll warn you before you leave. Anyone asking for a spell will get what they ask for, so don't take this magic lightly."

7   "Do it as a cock crows at dawn, make your wish, then leave without looking back."

8   "Make Mike Ayres' life come to an untimely end."

9   "If you look back, you will call down a terrible curse upon yourself."

10   "Now you see what you've done. I told you not to look back."

Come-Uppance

1   "I've lived with you for eleven long years and all that time you've messed with other women and it must stop!"

2   "If you don't stop, you'll see what will happen!"

Tricks of the Trade

1   "Somebody's 'obeah-ed' you."

2   "You have a duppy living in your tree, but don't worry, I can drive him away.

3   "You'll have no more trouble now."

To Divert The Course of Justice

1   "Things are not looking good... The police say they are going to get us."

2   "We're careless. I'm an idiot."

3   "You just do as I say and it will be alright on the day."

4   "Take the handkerchiefs when you go to court, wet them with Florida water and use them to wipe your faces, then come see me afterwards.

5   "Nothing, your Honour. It's hot in here, Sir."

6   "It's a warning."

7   "What's this noise all about?"

8   "Come on Gene. Let's go steal another goat."

An English Obeah Story

1   "What do you miss most?"

2   "The weather. I can't get used to the cold."

3   "You all know what I mean. You know how things are 'slow'. I miss the 'It will soon come' attitude. I miss the patois. They called me foreigner when I went home last year because of my English accent."

4   "The friendliness of the people and the nosiness. I love it man. We can't walk into somebody's house for food and gossip like back home. We are becoming like the British. We have to let people know that we're coming to see them. Even the food doesn't taste, for its not fresh like back home. I love my orange straight from the tree."

5   "Are you all trying to say that you've never been to Obeah man."

6 "I have no faith in doctors, because an Obeah woman gave me a herb that cleared up a problem that I was having with my potency."

7 "You must be daft. Where did you ever hear such a thing?"

8 "I don't know what you see in this devil nonsense."

9 "Whatever it is, it works man."

10 "Go away. It wouldn't work on a boil on my behind."

Cock On A Stick

1 "It's my husband Nurse, he won't leave me alone. Anyhow I must have my lot."

2 "I'll see what my husband says Nurse."

3 "I even talked to Albert. He said you cured his ulcer and you're a good Obeah woman."

4 "Are they rubbers (condoms) nurse?"

5 "My husband has never used them before, so he won't know what to do."

6 "See nurse. The same way that you showed me how to put it on the broom stick."

The Will

1 "Father has been good to us, so I'm gonna give him a good send off."

About the Author

David Brailsford was born in Nottingham, England in 1930. He was educated at the High Pavement Grammar School.

Qualifying as a Psychiatric Nurse in 1955, he progressed through his profession to become a Senior Nursing Officer, then developed a Staff in-house Training Department and worked with clients as a Registered Dramatherapist.

Now retired, he spends his time writing and telling stories, being a performer at the Nottingham Storyteller's Club.

He specialises in tales of ghosts, Anansi and witchcraft in Jamaica.

He visits Jamaica every year to research for material with his Jamaican born wife, Leonie, who is his inspiration.

He has three daughters and ten grandchildren and lives with Leonie in Nottingham, England.

Further details of his work can be seen on the websites:

http://www.duppyman.co.uk, http://www.lmhpublishing.com, http://www.amazon.com

෴

The Illustrator of this book, John Stilgoe was born in Liverpool, England, and being surrounded by comedians it was inevitable that he became a cartoonist interested in humorous illustration.

He graduated from the North Staffordshire Polytechnic with a BA (hons) in Fine Art and from Leicester Polytechnic with an Art Teacher's Diploma and a Post Graduate Certificate in Education. Currrently he is Head of Art Design and Technology at Hinckley High School.

His cartoons and illustrations have been used in advertising, training, promotions and presentations by industry, education and private individuals, which have included TTS Education supplies, the BMW Club Journal, Clarion Magazine and the RSPCA.

In 1999, John won first place for a single image gag at the Leicester Festival of Comedy.

John also illustrated David's first book of Jamaican Ghost Stories entitled Duppy Stories, then a book about the life of Anansi, Jamaica's folklore Spiderman hero, and will soon be collaborating on a book of children's stories.

Further information can be seen at www.johnstilgoe.co.uk

Other Books by the Author:

DUPPY STORIES

A collection of short stories about the ghosts that haunt Jamaica.

A potpourri of authentic stories, some 'true', some ugly and sinister and some amusing.

CONFESSIONS OF ANANSI

The *'autobiography'* of Jamaica's renowned hero, Anansi, the Spiderman. We are taken, with Anansi, to his life in Ghana; then onto a slave ship to Jamaica, where he travels through the island, meeting with other great heroes right up to the present day.

LaVergne, TN USA
05 December 2009
166013LV00006B/4/P